"Dear Peter Reich . . . But, my God! your book is beautiful! Important! Timely! Much closer to the bone of my contention than Castaneda."

—KEN KESEY

"An extraordinary memoir that stirs both mind and emotions long after one has read it. . . . The book, with its blend of dreams, memories, and mature filial reflections, is a rare and haunting literary achievement."

—*Publishers Weekly*

"The memoir . . . is a touching, eloquent, and curiously ambivalent mixture of juvenile memories, dreams, and adult questionings. . . . Fascinating."

—*Atlantic Monthly*

"Neither science nor fiction, *A Book of Dreams* inhabits its own special and highly vulnerable reality. The truth of what young Reich says he experienced is rooted in the timeless mysteries of fathers and sons, where the literal and the mythic cannot always be distinguished."

—*Time*

"i enjoyed reich's dreams very much."

—JOHN LENNON

"A delicate, wondrously imaginative piece of literature."

—*Tuscaloosa News*

"*A Book of Dreams* does not tell truths—it *is* truth, deep truth, enthralling truth about Peter Reich's childhood charged by his heroic, incandescent father, Wilhelm."

—MYRON R. SHARAF,
author of *Fury on Earth:*
A Biography of Wilhelm Reich

A BOOK OF
DREAMS

A BOOK OF DREAMS

A Memoir of Wilhelm Reich

PETER REICH

With a New Preface by
the Author

A Dutton Obelisk Paperback

E. P. DUTTON / NEW YORK

This paperback edition of *A Book of Dreams* first published in 1989 by E. P. Dutton

Copyright © 1973, 1989 by Peter Reich

Published in the United States by E. P. Dutton, a division of NAL Penguin Inc., 2 Park Avenue, New York, N.Y. 10016.

Published simultaneously in Canada by Fitzhenry and Whiteside, Limited, Toronto.

Library of Congress Catalog Card Number: 88-51772

ISBN: 0-525-48415-9

Designed by Gloria Adelson

10 9 8 7 6 5 4 3 2 1

Grateful acknowledgment is made for permission to quote lyrics from "Party Doll" by Buddy Knox and Jimmy Bower. Copyright © 1957 and 1958. Copyright renewed © 1985 and 1986 by Longitude Music Corp. All rights reserved. Reprinted by permission of Longitude Music Corp.

Preface

This book wrote itself in the summer of 1970.

Dusan Makavejev, the Yugoslavian filmmaker, had just left Rangeley, Maine, leaving me suspended between the reality of his film *WR: Mysteries of the Organism* and an inexpressible haze of troubling memories. The very day he left I stumbled upon an old abandoned dump in the woods. Peeling back a mossy blanket of pine needles and roots, I uncovered old glass, bottles, cans . . . and reels of old 16mm film.

The film was blue, and against the summer sky it flickered.

Then, Faulkner took over as psychic choreographer. *The Sound and the Fury* boiled in my imagination, providing a strange, intense relief from the nimble psychology of Makavejev who complained that everyone had a "blind spot" when it came to Reich. My blind spot was the child's eye, and Faulkner peeled it open. I stared through Caddy's, Benjy's, Quentin's eyes . . . and learned to speak. Closing the book, I walked to the typewriter, and my fingers began doing that strange dance over the keyboard.

Most of the childhood passages are virtually as they poured out, first draft. The memories were so keen and vivid that I was not conscious of any effort in writing . . . simply of moving fingers fast enough over the typewriter keyboard to keep up.

Some reviews took the book to task for hedging. They seemed to be saying, "You did a good job of telling us how it felt. You didn't tell us what you thought or think about it all."

To the boy it was total absorption for the first thirteen years in a true-life 1950s adventure with a sad ending. To the twenty-six-year-old writer it was breathtaking to be consumed so totally by the verbal expression of excruciatingly vivid memories and to see them take some meaningful shape on paper. To let words wrap themselves around the mysterious events of that turbulent childhood was pure liberation. So, the twenty-six-year-old really wasn't ready to think about it; he wanted to unload.

The forty-four-year-old husband and father is a private person to whom this all happened a long time ago. He waits, he watches. A critic once said that Wilhelm Reich had grabbed truth by more than its tail. How much more? Does anybody know? Does Orgone Energy exist? So, yes, the son is still hedging. Perhaps the story, released now and no longer a secret, generates some energy of its own.

I owe a lot to Caddy (and her creator) who showed me that I could "close the covers on it and even the weightless hand of a child could put it back among its unfeatured kindred on the quiet eternal shelves and turn the key upon it for the whole and dreamless night."

SEPTEMBER, 1988

Part one

Chapter 1

I, the dreamer clinging yet to the dream as the patient clings to the last thin unbearable ecstatic instant of agony in order to sharpen the savor of the pain's surcease, waking into the reality, the more than reality, not to the unchanged and unaltered old time but into a time altered to fit the dream which, conjunctive with the dreamer, becomes immolated and apotheosized.

WILLIAM FAULKNER in *Absalom! Absalom!*

Half a deer walked up to my house and rattled at the door. When I didn't answer, the deer went away and I watched him turn into a whole deer. He walked away into trees where the wind was watery voices of people I did not know.

Strange watery voices were all I could hear. I could not see because I was my eyes, my eyes were crying so hard because I was so afraid.

In the voices they were talking about the deer. I went out of the house when the deer was gone. The lawn was soggy long grass that lay in thick strands like washed hair. I was surprised that the lake had climbed the hill to the cabin. The water, rising up the hill, was cloudy and bright yellow as if the sun were caught beneath it.

As I ranged up and down the shores of the swollen lake I saw a man's feet floating beneath the surface. The bottoms of his feet were near the surface and sometimes small waves broke over them. The rest of the man disappeared beneath the water.

When I opened my eyes, doctors and nurses were moving around me talking in a strange language. A white sheet was over me. Oh, Jesus Christ, I've been in a dream and suddenly I'm waking up in a strange place. I don't know who I am or where I am or what is happening. What is that language?

I closed my eyes but all there was to see was water so I opened them again. But I didn't see differently or know more. Sometime, a long time ago, something must have happened and I got amnesia, and now I am waking up in this hospital—is it a mental hospital? There was a mental hospital somewhere. . . .

My arm began to hurt so I lay back on the table and tried to relax and remember as much as I could:

I was born in New York City on April 3, 1944. My mother and father, Ilse Ollendorff and Wilhelm Reich, lived at 9906 Sixty-ninth Avenue in Forest Hills. The telephone number was Boulevard 8–5997. We lived there for a long time and then we moved to Maine. My father was a psychiatrist. When we moved to Maine he bought a big tract of land and called it Orgonon. He discovered Orgone Energy, which was Life Energy. He did a lot of experiments with it and lots of other doctors and scientists came to help. The big thing was the accumulator. It was like a box and you sat in it and it made you feel better. I was happy then. A lot of people said my father was a quack. A lot of bad things happened I can't remember. . . .

The doctor came over and spoke to me in a funny language. He said something about gas. . . .

Wait. My parents were separated. My father died. I went to a Quaker boarding school. Then I went to college in Maine and took my junior year abroad. . . . Yes, that was it, I was remembering. I was in France. Those people were speaking French.

I was in France, now, in 1963, and there had been an accident. I had gone to Geneva with a friend who had a motorcycle. We stayed overnight in a youth hostel and went to visit the United Nations palace the next day. Then we started back to Grenoble and coming around a hairpin curve we went off the road. That was why my shoulder hurt: I had dislocated my shoulder.

That was why there was pain and why I was in the hospital afraid to close my eyes because of the water. There was a dream in the gas.

The doctor came back again and smiled. He said they had not been able to get my shoulder back in its socket and would have to give me gas again. Again? Had I already been through some dream? The mask came over my face slowly and it was sickening and familiar. This has happened before and before. There *is* another dream. There was an incredible dream I had that no one would ever believe. The gas was sweet as I tried to remember and already one had passed and two was coming because I was a soldier in a war long ago but no one would ever believe three or four and already it was racing down a purple corridor with neon numbers clicking on and off in the trillions spinning all the way through the purple ribbon until out of it a thin black ribbon bent around the side of my head, encircled it, grew wider and wider and because no one would believe what happened was all black.

So I finally made sergeant. It was 1954.

Tightening the white plastic Sam Browne belt around my waist and over my chest, I adjusted the shiny new sergeant's badge over my heart and looked down the road. A car was coming so I blew the whistle.

On either side of me, a few yards down the road, privates swung their wrists, leaning two stop signs out into the road. The car stopped.

I lifted my white sergeant's pole, swung it around in front of me and looked at the third-grader standing next to me. "Okay," I said.

We walked to the other side. I swung the pole around and let the third-grader walk up the asphalt pathway to Edward L. Wetmore School. Beyond the low school building, children were playing on a large dusty playfield.

I walked back across the road and blew the whistle again. The two stop signs swung back and the car drove past.

As soon as he got his sign up, Rudy yelled at me. "Hey, stupid, you're not supposed to hold the white pole in front of you. It is supposed to be in the direction you're going!"

Rudy was mad at me because I made sergeant before he did. But he didn't try as hard as I did. Ray Urbelejo made lieutenant. He's my friend.

"I'll do it any way I want to."

Actually, I was a sergeant before, but nobody knew about that. Ray and Rudy wouldn't understand. I'm a lieutenant too, in the cavalry, and my scout is named Toreano, but they wouldn't understand that either. I'm a lieutenant when I wear the Stetson and a sergeant when I wear the pith helmet. As soon as we got to Tucson, Bill and I called Daddy, because he was still coming in his car with Eva. I asked him if I could buy a real cowboy hat and he said okay. So we went to Jacome's and bought a real Stetson for $12. It's a real cowboy hat. Then when Daddy arrived and our expedition began, he bought pith helmets for all of us and I got a red crayon and painted sergeant's stripes on it. Bill Moise, my brother-in-law, is a lieutenant and we're cosmic engineers. But Ray and Rudy wouldn't understand.

"Hey, stupid, there's a car coming!" Rudy looked at me impatiently as I blew the whistle.

As soon as we were relieved, I went back up to the locker room to hang up my belt and go out to look for popsicle sticks before the bell rang. Ray had finished checking off the white belts so we went outside together to look for popsicle sticks. We walked to the jungle jim where most of the kids ate their popsicles and started picking them up. Ray was asking me about Maine because I told him that was where I came from.

"Do you really get a lot of snow up there?"

"Yeah, once it was up to my waist. We used to have great snowball fights in school."

I sat down and started to jam the first bunch of sticks into my engineer boots. Ray sat down next to me.

"Gee, I've never seen snow. Can you eat it?"

I shifted the popsicle sticks so they were all even, all the way around my leg. "Yeah, you can when you get thirsty, but actually, it just makes you more thirsty. It's not good to eat too much of it."

"Wow, someday I'd like to get up there and see it. My dad, uh, travels and maybe we could get up there sometime." He jiggled his boot to let the popsicle sticks settle. He wore cowboy boots. They were higher and he could get more sticks in his.

We got up and started looking around for more sticks. We walked over to the swings, where kids dropped their feet into the dust on the downswing and made puffs of smoke. We picked up popsicle sticks until our boots were stuffed up to the top and then we took out our yoyos. Ray did some around-the-horns and I just let mine sleep for a while. We yoyoed for a while watching dust devils sweep across the playground.

"Hey," said Ray, "I thought you had one of these glow-in-the-dark yoyos." He swung his red glow-in-the-darker around the world and dropped into a baby's cradle.

My black diamond Duncan flipped back into my hand after a double around-the-horn.

"Yeah, well, you see, my dad said I had to get rid of it on account of the glow-in-the-dark stuff."

"Huh?"

"Well, you see, he works with some radioactive stuff and he

told me that the glow-in-the-dark on the yoyo and his radioactive stuff don't mix. It might make me sick or something."

"Wow, that sounds eerie. What kind of stuff does your dad do?" He dropped his yoyo into a long sleep. I swung my yoyo around the world and when it got back, walked the doggy.

"Well, actually, we're on an atmospheric research expedition."

"An expedition? Wow!" He flipped his yoyo back into his hand.

"Yeah, and you see we've got this machine called a cloudbuster —but it really isn't a machine—and we use it to make rain. My dad, he decided to come down here and break the drought." Daddy always said not to brag, but I was just telling. A lump of popsicle sticks dropped around my ankles. I stopped to hike them up and Ray swung around the world.

"You mean you can really make it rain?"

"Sure. Last year when we were back East, in Maine, there was a drought, and all the blueberries were drying up. You know, that's where they grow blueberries."

"Yeah?" He palmed his yoyo and listened.

"Yeah. So these blueberry growers heard about the cloudbuster and called my dad up. They said they'd give him ten thousand dollars to make it rain."

"Wowee," said Ray, shaking his head. "Ten thousand bucks is a lot of money. Did you make it rain?"

I swung around the horn. It wasn't bragging, it was just telling the truth. Besides, I'd never tell him about the flying saucers.

"Yup, twenty-four hours after we worked the cloudbuster, it started the rain. The weather bureau had said there wouldn't be any rain for a couple of days and then, wham." The yoyo slapped back into my hand just as the bell rang and we started back toward the school building.

"Well, gee, your dad must be pretty rich then, if he can go around making rain for money, especially out here." He grinned.

"Well, we're not really rich. You see, there's a problem with the government."

"The government?"

"Yeah. They don't believe it works, so they're giving my dad a hard time about it . . . it's kind of complicated."

"Wow. Well, do you think I could come over sometime and look at the cloudthing?"

"Yeah, I guess so."

Swarms of kids walked past us as we went down the outside corridor that ran past the classrooms. Little dunes of dust had gathered in front of the doors.

"What does your dad do?" I asked.

Ray's face turned a little red. "Aaw, he just works on farms and stuff."

I started wheeling in my yoyo. "But there aren't that many farms around here, are there? What kind of farms?"

Ray shoved his yoyo into his jeans pocket. "Well, you see, we actually kind of, well, go out on the road, you know? Like probably before the end of school my dad will take me and my brothers and sisters and we'll probably go up to California or Washington and pick stuff up there."

"You mean you are going to have to leave school in order to help your dad work?"

"Yeah. See, you notice how I'm kind of older than the rest of the kids in the class?"

"Yeah?"

"Well, see, we got to leave every year because there's no work around here. So I miss a lot of school. Then when I get back, well, I'm behind a grade. Actually I should be in eighth grade."

"Wow." I didn't know what to say. The schools were so much easier in Tucson that as soon as I started, I had skipped a grade, so I was in fifth grade now.

"Well, gee, Ray, maybe if my dad's cloudbuster works,

it'll rain down here and then there'll be crops and you won't have to leave."

He grinned and with a hand on the doorknob ready to go into class, he said, "Yeah, yeah, that'd be all right."

And I thought that if we stayed friends, maybe I could tell him about the flying saucers.

We sat on the last seat of the schoolbus going home playing tic-tac-toe in the suede on the back of my cowboy jacket with the fringes on it. I stretched the jacket over my books and smoothed it one way with my hand so we could make a tic-tac-toe cross going the other way. Ray heaped his denim jacket over his knee and made an x. Then I made an o and he made another x. I made an o and he beat me with the next x.

"That sure is a nice jacket," he said, smoothing out the suede and making another tic-tac-toe cross.

"Yeah, some friends gave it to me before I came out West. I got a horse too. . . ." I stopped. That was bragging. Ray didn't say anything, he just beat me at another game of tic-tac-toe. I looked at his faded denim jacket. It had army patches on it, with all different colors and designs. I wanted to get some of those too. Sometimes Daddy and I talked about a flag and insignia for the Cosmic Engineers. Someday we might even get uniforms.

"Hey, Ray, where'd you get all the patches?"

"Well, I got the first ones when my brother was in the army. Then there's a kid who sells 'em at school real cheap."

"I'd like to get some."

"Yeah, but you couldn't put them on your suede jacket, could you?"

"Oh yeah." Maybe I could get Daddy to buy me a denim jacket like Ray's. After letting Ray off, the bus made a few more stops and then swung back onto the main road for a while before it turned onto our road. I got my jacket and boots together and walked up to the front of the bus when we got near our ranch.

The bus driver was a big strong man with curly blond hair. He looked like the kind of muscle men they showed at the end of comic books, and the muscles in his arms rippled as he steered around the last corner before our place. I leaned down and saw the cluster of pipes from the cloudbuster sticking up between the hard green Palo Verde leaves. The bus stopped right by the gate and instead of opening the door, the driver turned around and looked at me.

"Hey," he said, "I've been meaning to ask you. What is that thing with the pipes?" The lines around his nose dropped into a sneer around his mouth.

"We call it a cloudbuster," I said, starting down the steps to get off.

"A clodbuster?" He grinned. There was a black space between two of his teeth. He turned away, leaned forward on the steering wheel and looked back at the cloudbuster. From where the bus was he could see the whole truck with the platform on the back, the black square base, the cables leading up to the pipes and the spinning wave on the side of the truck. He nodded. "A clodbuster, huh?"

"No," I said, "a cloudbuster."

"Well, uh, what do they use this clodbuster for?" He held one hand on the door opening lever like he wouldn't open until I told him.

"Uh, we use it for atmospheric research. Can I get out, please?"

"Atmospheric research? Ha. What's that?" He grinned.

"Well, uh, it is for an experiment in weather control." I stepped down until I was right in front of the door.

He nodded and grinned again. "Oh, I see. That there clodbuster controls the weather, huh? Well, just don't bust any of my clods. Ha ha." His big hand pulled back on the lever and the door swung open. I stepped down into the dust. He held the door open and looked at me with his mouth open. Then he said, "Well, take it easy, clodbuster," and slammed the door.

The bus started down the road in a cloud of dust and I watched it get smaller and smaller. He made me feel bad. That was why I had to be brave. It was emotional plague.

When the bus was gone, I turned and walked across the rail fence and down the driveway to the ranch. Daddy called it Little Orgonon but I didn't like it as much as Orgonon. The cloudbuster was off to the side of the driveway. Painted on the door was the big red spinning wave that Daddy always talked about. I didn't understand it but he said it was the key to how the flying saucers worked.

Hobbling on account of the popsicle sticks in my boots, I walked down the driveway toward the house. When I got to the Palo Verde tree next to the kitchen I pulled off my boots and spilled the popsicle sticks into two piles on the ground. Daddy's car wasn't there so I'd have time to work before he got back.

I felt around in the sand near the base of the tree until I found the buried metal plate. I dug the sand away from the plate and lifted it up. Beneath it was a small hole in the ground. I reached into the hole carefully, because there might be scorpions, and took out a small bundle wrapped in black banana skins. I laid the bundle on the metal plate and slowly unwrapped the bright green glow-in-the-dark yoyo. It was a beautiful bright yoyo and I was sorry I couldn't play with it. I slipped the loop over my finger to do a few whirls with it but then I remembered that Daddy said it was bad for me. I put it back onto the metal plate and went into the kitchen for water. I poured the water into the hole to loosen up the dirt and then I started digging.

Daddy said I had to bury the glow-in-the-dark yoyo because the glow stuff was deadly just like fluorescent light. Glow-in-the-dark light was bad energy and it didn't mix with Orgone Energy, which was good energy. Daddy was trying to kill the bad energy in the atmosphere. Bad energy came from flying saucers and bombs. The cloudbuster cleaned the atmosphere of the deadly orgone—we called it DOR—and fought the flying saucers. Only we called the flying saucers EAs. It was initials. The E stood for something and the A stood for something. Daddy told me what it was but I forgot. We had names for a lot of stuff. The EAs' energy was like glow-in-the-dark energy and it made us sick.

We were all sensitive to strange energy things, especially my sister Eva. Fluorescent light was really bad, and Eva could never understand how people survived in office buildings with dead light energy. The same with glow-in-the-dark watch dials or television. It got so that Eva could tell if someone was wearing a glow-in-the-dark watch just by feeling the energy around him. She could feel TV that way too and it made her sick. She was the one who spotted my green glow-in-the-dark yoyo. One day when I came near her she felt funny and got a little green herself. She asked me what I was wearing and where I had been. Then I took out the glow-in-the-dark yoyo and started yoyoing and she almost fainted. That was when Daddy said I had to bury it.

The wet sand had made a dark slippery pile next to me and I had to reach almost all the way up to my shoulder to reach the end of it. When it was long enough, I hollowed it out for a while to make it bigger and then I moved the popsicle sticks over closer. Just like in the old gold mines in the westerns, I started putting them against the walls and on the ceiling, lining the hole just like a real gold mine. It was really exciting making the mine and thinking that maybe someday someone would be digging there and find it. It was the kind of adventure that Ray wouldn't understand at all. After a while I noticed that I was actually starting to feel a little sick too just from being so close to the yoyo.

Sometimes I thought Eva was feeling too much with the TV sets and the glow-in-the-dark watches, but I'd been observing more and more and I wasn't really sure.

The first thing Daddy said once he and Eva arrived in

Tucson and I had showed him my new Stetson was that we all had to have an unrigid way of feeling and observing. Like before we used the cloudbuster, we always waited for a while, and looked at the sky to see what was there and what we felt. To use the cloudbuster you had to know how the sky felt and we got pretty good at it. Sometimes, on a day when we all felt bad, even if we were far apart, we found out later that there was an atomic-bomb explosion or an EA attack.

The EA attacks and the atomic-bomb explosions coincided with bad DOR, and we could tell because every time the sky was ugly brownish grey and people felt bad and looked bad, we found out that there had been a bomb. The cloudbuster made the atmosphere and people feel better. Sort of like the accumulator only bigger. And we were the only people who knew about it.

Just as I put the last popsicle sticks into the tunnel, I heard a car and Daddy drove up. He parked in front of the house and walked over to where I was working.

"Hi, Peeps," he said. "What are you doing? Did you have a good day?"

"Yeah. I'm burying the yoyo like you said."

"Good. It is very dangerous to have that around. You must be careful of toys like that. This happened before, don't you remember?"

"But I still don't understand why I have to *bury* it," I said, putting the yoyo, rewrapped in banana skins, all the way to the end of the gold-mine tunnel.

"I have told you, Peeps, that the glow-in-the-dark paint has a negative charge. It is like fluorescent light. Do you know the glass bulb I have in my car?" Taped to the back window of his car, Daddy had a small glass vacuum bulb with a little vane-like propeller in it. On one side the vanes were white and on the other side they were black. He said it was a miniature model of an Orgone motor. I nodded. "Well, you know that Orgone Energy makes the propeller turn around. DOR slows it down. That is why it turns faster on bright days and slower on bad days. But it won't turn at all under fluorescent light or the kind of glow-in-the-dark light of your yoyo. Rather than giving off energy, it draws it away, absorbs it, from living things."

"How come the other kids don't get sick then?" I began patting the dark wet sandmud into the hole, sealing the glow-in-the-dark yoyo forever.

"But they are, Pete. They are tightly armored against feeling the deep effects of DOR sickness. They fight it off with toughness and dirty jokes but the sickness still eats them away inside. Their faces become tight and their jaws get rigid because they no longer feel. When they get older, they die of cancer. Sometimes I see armoring in you and that is why I give you treatments."

"All their bellies are hard?"

"Yes. And their way of achieving things is a hard-bellied way. Do you remember the movie we saw with John Wayne, in which he falls and becomes crippled?"

"The one where he plays a navy officer. Yeah. He fell down stairs at night and the doctors told him he would never walk again."

"Ja. You see, when he was sitting in bed, looking down to the end of his cast watching his toes, he resolved to walk again. And he said, over and over again, 'Gonna move that toe, gonna move that toe, gonna move that toe.' You see, that is the rigid way of overcoming things."

I patted the last of the mud over the tunnel, placed the metal plate over the opening, and spread dry dust over the top. Then I stood up and walked with Daddy toward the house.

"But in the end, he walked, didn't he?" I asked.

"Yes, but you see, to overcome obstacles that way, by force, so-called will power, that is communist. It is the rigid, mechanistic way of accomplishing things. He had to make himself so tight and hard to force himself to walk again that he forgot how to love and be kind."

"And it would have been better if he had had Orgone Therapy, right? Then he would have walked and still been a good person."

"Ja, very good, Peeps. The best way is just to breathe, and relax, and let it come naturally. Never force anything, just let it be natural, and it will always be okay. Okay?" He smiled at me and I nodded.

"Now," he said, "how would you like to go to the Green Lantern and have some special swordfish for dinner?"

"I'd love it," I said.

I ran in the house and washed my hands. Daddy was waiting in the car and as we drove out the driveway I remembered the bus driver.

"Daddy, I have to make a report."

"What is it?"

"Well, today, coming back on the schoolbus the bus driver made a bunch of funny remarks about the cloudbuster. He called it a clodbuster and laughed at me when I told him it was for atmospheric research."

Daddy looked serious. "Don't let him get to you, Pete. He may be a spy trying to find out what we're up to, or he may just be a sick person. Whatever you do, just be brave and remember that his type are the killers, the real carriers of emotional plague. You will run into them wherever you go. Did you tell him anything else?"

"No, I just told him that it is a cloudbuster and we use it for weather control. He just called it 'clodbuster' and told me not to bust any clods."

"He sounds like he was just being afraid. Don't worry about him. Many people are afraid. Like those television people who came here and took movies about the cloudbuster for a newsreel. They were interested at first because we spoke about weather control and rainmaking and then, mysteriously, the film was ruined. There are many mysterious things happening. . . ."

"But the grass isn't mysterious," I said, looking out the window at the desert on the road going in to Tucson. "They'll see when they really see the grass."

"Ja," said Daddy, "today I drove nearly sixty miles out into the country around Tucson, talking to farmers and cowboys. They all say that they have never seen such nice rich grass growing in a long time. Yes, they won't laugh when it rains in the desert and makes grass grow."

The Green Lantern had a big organ sitting on a platform near the mirror-backed wooden bar, and red yellow and green lights went around in circles over the organist, making his face change colors. The spotlight shone through colored disks and its light reflected in the bar mirror across the dining room as if it were shining on me and Daddy sitting in our favorite booth. Daddy was smiling at me as he sipped his favorite drink, a Manhattan.

"Do you want the cherry?" He stirred his drink with it, holding it by the stem. It blurred as it went around and around. Daddy always remembered to give me the cherry from his Manhattan.

"Yes." He handed it to me and it was sweet and strong, and made my breath feel heavy. Daddy motioned to the waitress who usually served us and she came over to take our orders. She was pretty and had bright eyes and she always made a fuss over me. She leaned over and tousled my hair, laughing. "Hi there, how are you tonight?"

My face got hot. I looked away "Oh, all right, I guess." She smiled and looked at Daddy.

"He is so cute," she said.

Daddy laughed and nodded, and then he said, "I'll have shrimp and Pete will have swordfish."

She took it down and went away, in a wind of perfume and organ music.

Daddy finished his drink and looked at me.

"Do you have a girl friend?" he asked.

He always wanted to know if I had a girl friend and if we

kissed or touched each other. He always said, "Don't be afraid to talk to me." So we talked a lot about why I wasn't circumcised and what other kids were like. There was a girl at school who was very pretty and we looked at each other in a secret way sometimes, but we hadn't kissed.

"Well," I said, "there is a girl I like but we don't go out or anything." It made me embarrassed to talk about it, and actually, I had a lot of fun on road patrol and playing yoyo.

"Daddy, I was talking to my friend Ray today and I told him a little bit about the cloudbuster. That's okay, isn't it?"

"Yes, but you must be careful not to say too much."

"Oh, I didn't tell him about the flying saucers or anything. We just talked about making rain and stuff. His dad works on farms and since it doesn't rain here, he has to go far away to get work."

"Ja. That is interesting, because I think we shall be able to bring rain to Tucson, finally, and break the drought. Then your friend's father wouldn't have to go away."

"And maybe Ray could come and be a cosmic engineer with us."

Daddy smiled and leaned back while the waitress came with our plates and served the food. She leaned very close to me and winked at me. I smiled and looked away.

"Will there be anything else?" She smiled at us.

Daddy said no, and she said, "Well, if you need anything, just let me know. I'll be keeping an eye on you." She winked at me again and was gone.

The swirling lights went around and around in the mirror over the organ.

"Daddy, why is there a desert in the first place?" I squeezed the lemon over my swordfish, and began eating.

"At first I wasn't sure," he said. "Driving out here I saw vegetation dying everywhere. It was clear that something was attacking the atmosphere. At first I just thought it was a natural phenomenon, much like dry spots in the human body, and that the cloudbuster, like the accumulator, could get it moving again. But then I began to wonder if it wasn't the EAs that caused the desert. Now I think that fallout from the bombs they are testing makes DOR too. All the DOR from the EAs and the bombs is slowly killing the earth's envelope of Orgone Energy."

"Is that why we always take rock samples and wood samples?"

"That's very good, Peeps. Exactly. When the DOR became very concentrated, the rocks around Orgonon began to crumble. You remember we looked at the rocks on the observatory together and saw them crumble. That was just an example of how the healthy atmosphere is being destroyed."

"Do the EAs know about Orgone Energy?"

"I think so. I think they use Orgone Energy for fuel. That would explain why they are silent and that silver-blue color. It would also explain why they respond when we draw with the Orur."

Daddy had an experiment called Oranur. He put a radium needle in a big accumulator but something bad happened. Instead of making good energy it made bad energy. It also made the needle very charged and sometimes we used it on the cloudbuster. It made the cloudbuster stronger.

I squeezed more lemon on my swordfish. We ate for a while and then Daddy said, "Peeps, I know this is all a great deal for you to understand. If you ever become afraid or want to leave, tell me, and you can go back to Mummy. I know it is very difficult for you, for we are not only being attacked by the government, but now by flying saucers. You must be brave, sonny."

Daddy said things were building up to a big battle but I wasn't scared. I was a sergeant in the Corps of Cosmic Engineers with sergeants' stripes on my pith helmet and a qualified operator of the cloudbuster.

"I'm not afraid, Daddy. I mean, the Air Force is on our side, isn't it?"

After Daddy began making reports to the Air Force about

his work with the EAs, Air Force jets came over Orgonon a lot more, sometimes real close, sometimes far away.

When they were high in the sky, they left long white vapor trails. After a while Daddy said he thought the Air Force was helping him by telling him where the DOR in the atmosphere was, because where the DOR was bad, the jet vapor trails disintegrated quickly, and when there was good Orgone Energy, they stayed for a long time.

Daddy was really sure the Air Force knew and understood what he was doing, and on the way out West, Bill and I stopped at Wright Patterson Air Force Base to talk to a general about the flying saucers. But the general wouldn't see him and he had to see someone else.

"Ahem, ahem ahem," said Daddy, finishing his shrimp. "I think the Air Force understands, but for some reason they still can't help. They seemed so interested in what we were doing at first and then all of a sudden there was nothing, even though their jets continued to fly over Orgonon. That sudden cutting off . . . it is very much like the Einstein affair . . . sometimes it all seems like a conspiracy. The changing attitude runs through everything like a red thread." He shook his head.

"What Einstein thing?"

He looked at me thoughtfully and shook his head again. "Nothing, Peeps, nothing. I was just thinking. Would you like some ice cream?"

"Yup. Coffee and strawberry."

"Okay." He waved at the waitress. She came over and while Daddy ordered the ice cream I went over to the man on the organ sitting beneath the bright colored lights. He was big and fat and smelled like a cigar. When I stood next to the organ he leaned over and winked at me.

"Hey there, young fella," he said. "Is there a special song you'd like me to play?"

I nodded. "Do you know the song from *She Wore a Yellow Ribbon*?"

"I sure do. Why? Do you like that song?"

"Yup," I said proudly. "I saw it five times and the fifth time I got in free."

"Well, in that case I'll have to play it for you." He gave me a big grin and a slap on the back.

In the mirror, Daddy looked at me and smiled. Then he nodded to the organ man and the organ man nodded back. I went back to the table and started eating ice cream and the organ man started playing "She Wore a Yellow Ribbon."

The ice cream was good. As I ate it I listened to the song and watched the organ lights spin through different colors onto the organ man. I thought about Toreano, my scout, and our cavalry fort at Orgonon. I had decided to leave Toreano in charge because it was too far for him to come to Arizona. It was fall and Toreano would be out riding his pony across the rainy fields, guarding Orgonon.

The waitress came and sat down next to me in the booth. She put her arm around me and squeezed her breast into my shoulder. It felt good but I didn't know what to do.

"Do you like this song?" she asked, squeezing.

I nodded and scooped the last of the ice cream out of the dish. Daddy was watching us and smiling.

"I bet you're a good cowboy," she said. "And I bet you're fast on the draw, aren't you?"

I nodded and she laughed, squeezing me again.

"Well, if you ever need a good cowgirl, just let me know." She smiled at Daddy and slipped out of the booth, picking up the money Daddy had put on the check. Smiling at both of us, she said, "Thanks, now, and you come again," and went away. On the way out of the restaurant, we waved at the organist and as we got into the car, Daddy chuckled.

"Do you know why that waitress was flirting with you?" he asked.

"Is it because she likes me?"

"Well, of course she likes you," said Daddy, "but the real reason is that she wants to make love to me and she doesn't know how to come out and say it. So she lets her love out on you."

"Oh." Daddy always knew what people were doing and what they were thinking. Once we were sitting in a restaurant and all of a sudden Daddy poked me in the ribs. He nodded to a couple sitting a few tables away with their backs to us. "In a minute," said Daddy, "that man will turn around and stare at me." Daddy looked back at his plate but I kept looking around the room as if I were not looking at anyone in particular and sure enough in a few seconds the man turned around very slowly and gave Daddy a long, mean look. When he turned back around, I whispered to Daddy, "How come you knew he would do that?" And Daddy smiled. "A few minutes ago his wife was flirting with me, looking at me and smiling. As soon as I smiled back, she turned and said something to her husband. I am sure she said, 'Turn around and look at that strange man who is staring at us,' because he did."

But I couldn't figure out why the waitress was flirting with me unless it was because she liked me.

When we got home, I started to do some long division but it was hard and I felt like there might be an EA or something in the air, so I went outside and up on the observation platform.

I stood there for a long time switching from telescope to binoculars, looking for flying saucers. On really dark nights we could see the rings around Saturn and Jupiter's moons and it was funny to watch them and then hear a coyote in the hills or a long train rumbling along toward Tucson. Sometimes we saw an EA to the southwest of Tucson. It was a pulsating red-and-green ball hovering in the sky. It came so regularly that we called it the Southern Belle. Sometimes it went back and forth, sometimes it got brighter and dimmer and sometimes it moved fast across the sky, dodging the draw of the cloudbuster.

I was just about to go back downstairs to my long division when I saw it, hovering in the south. I watched it for a minute. It pulsated and glowed. Then I ran down to get Daddy.

He was sitting in his work room at a long desk writing in one of his big red ledger books. It felt like a cavalry movie walking in and reporting.

"Daddy, I spotted one. In the east. It looks pretty big. I think it's the Southern Belle."

He pushed his chair back and stood up. "Let's go and look."

We both went up on the roof and Daddy looked at it for a long time through his binoculars. Ahem. AHEM ahem.

"Peter. Go downstairs and call Bill and Eva. Tell them to come over immediately. We are going to operate."

I raced downstairs and into the house. As soon as Bill answered, I said, "Bill, it's an EA. Daddy says to come over right away. We're going to operate."

When I got back upstairs, Daddy was looking through the telescope. "Here, look through. See if you can see. I can make out a thin cigar shape with little windows."

I looked through the telescope and focused it. It was bright, bright blue and glowing, but I couldn't see the windows.

"Do you see it?"

"Yeah, but I can't see the windows."

"Well, they are there. Run to the cloudbuster and make ready. Unplug all the pipes and pull them out to full length. I'll be right there."

My boots pounded against the dry dirt. My jacket was open, and each time my arms went back the sides of the jacket flapped against me and the fringes sounded like rain. As soon as I got to the cloudbuster I jumped up on the platform and started unplugging. The pipes were like an old-fashioned telescope and had two more sections inside that pulled out. Bill and Eva drove up just as I pulled out the last pipe. They parked near the truck.

Bill pulled his binoculars out of the case and put the strap over his neck. "Where is it?" he asked.

I pointed to it and Bill raised the glasses. He whistled.

"Boy, it sure is something," he said, handing the glasses to Eva.

She looked for a while and said, "I knew it would come. I felt bad all day and said to Bill that I thought there was something in the atmosphere."

We stood there waiting for Daddy to come, and I felt good and excited, as if we were about to do something adventurous and secret. I wished that Ray could see me, about ready to draw from a flying saucer. But he'd never believe it. He wouldn't understand.

Daddy came down the road with his big grey Stetson soft in the starlight.

"Ah. You came quickly. Good. Let's get to work."

Bill got up on the platform and the rest of us stood near the side of the truck. It wasn't good to be too close for too long.

Daddy said, "All right, Moise. Direct the pipes at the EA."

The little rubber plugs at the end of the pipes swung gently as Bill cranked the wheels around so that the pipes were pointing right at the cloudbuster. We waited. It didn't do anything. Sometimes they went from side to side when we started drawing, other times they'd just get fainter and fainter as if they were on the end of some long yoyo string being pulled back into the sky. Bill usually did the drawing but I did it too.

"I feel terrible," said Eva. "I can feel it reacting already. I get that salty taste in my mouth."

"Ja. I feel it too," said Daddy. "Do you feel anything, Moise?"

"Mmhmm," said Bill, "I can feel it starting in my stomach a bit."

"I've got a kind of choking feeling in my throat," I said.

Ahem. AHEM ahem. Daddy took off his hat and pushed his hand through his long silvery hair. "I wish I knew if this was an attack or if they are just observing Earth and don't know what they are doing."

We all watched the EA, sparkling blue, growing brighter, then dimmer, then bright again.

After a while, Daddy said, "Pete."

"Yes."

"You know where the Orur needle is kept, ja? Go and get it. Make sure you carry it very carefully. There is a flashlight in the truck."

It was scary walking down past the shadowy, dark cactus, but the flashlight helped. The needle was hidden under a little pile of rocks in a dry river bed. I took a couple of rocks off and shined the light against the dull lead container. The needle was inside, tied to a string that hung over the side. I picked up the end of the string and holding it as far in front of me as I could, I went back to the cloudbuster.

"Here it is," I said.

"Good," said Daddy. "Now hand it carefully to Moise. Ja. Good." There was another lead bottle right at the base of the cloudbuster where the metal cables came up to the pipes.

"How do you feel?" asked Daddy. Bill said he was okay but Eva said she had to go back to the house. She was supersensitive to Orurizing.

Bill kept the cloudbuster trained on the EA but it didn't go away. I was itching to get up and try it because I had an idea that might work.

"Daddy, can I relieve Bill?"

"Ja. It might be good. He has been up there a long time. Take a rest, Moise."

I climbed on the truck and stood next to Bill for a minute feeling like John Wayne or Clark Gable or somebody taking the controls from Robert Mitchum or William Holden.

"How is she going?" I asked.

Bill kept his eye on the EA. "Well, I'm just holding pretty steady on her."

"Okay."

Bill got down with Daddy and they both stood next to the

cloudbuster with their binoculars trained on the EA. I had one hand on each wheel, one for making the pipes go up and one for making them go down.

"Moise," said Daddy, "please go to the car and get the Geiger counter. I want to see how much the count has risen with the EA."

While Bill went for the Geiger counter, I tried my idea. I figured that if the cloudbuster could sort of take the energy away or weaken it, I could make the EA sort of fall by drawing underneath it and to either side of it, weakening the energy around it. So I moved the cloudbuster slowly from one side of the EA to the other. I let it draw on the right side for a while and then dipped slowly under it like a baby's cradle on a yoyo and rubbed back and forth at the sky beneath it before coming back up the other side. I let the cloudbuster Orurize on either side.

Bill came back with the Geiger counter and held his flashlight over the dial while Daddy flicked the switches.

"Incredible," said Daddy. "Such a high count cannot come only from the Orur. It can come only from the EA or the atmosphere. It is almost as if we are directly in the path of the exhaust from the EA. Maybe it is the exhaust which is causing the desert, sucking away all the moisture."

Bill agreed. "It seems consistent with your theory that Orgone Energy could neutralize fallout in a nuclear attack. If the EA's exhaust is DOR just like fallout creates DOR, then the cloudbuster could be the answer to the desert and the dying atmosphere."

"Ja. The atmosphere is always so clear and fresh after Orurizing. If we can stop the disintegration of the atmosphere and bring rain over from the Pacific we will break the drought and prove our point. Then the Air Force will understand. But look! The count has gone way down! Where is the EA?"

They looked up at the sky. "Why, it's gone," said Bill, searching the horizon with his binoculars.

I grinned. My idea had worked.

"What are you doing with the cloudbuster?" asked Daddy.

"I've been doing this. Watch." I moved the cloudbuster back and forth and up and down, checking through the sighting scope. Sure enough, the EA was just a faint glimmer and seemed to be getting smaller and smaller as if it was being sucked up by the sky.

When it was gone and we were putting the pipes back together, Daddy said, "That was very good, Peeps, very good. You are a real good little soldier because you have discovered a new way to disable the EAs. I am very proud of you."

After I put the needle away in the dry river bed and Bill had finished putting the rubber stoppers in the cloudbuster, we all walked back to the house together. I walked between Bill and Daddy. Daddy had his hand around my shoulder.

"Yes," he said, "we are really engaged in a cosmic war. Peeps, you must be very brave and very proud, for we are the first human beings to engage in a battle to the death with spaceships. We know now that they are destroying our atmosphere, perhaps by drawing off Orgone Energy as fuel, or by emitting DOR as exhaust. Either way, we are the only ones who understand what they are doing to the atmosphere and we can fight them on their own ground. The Air Force can only issue misleading reports about the flying saucers and chase after them helplessly, while we are dealing with them functionally, with Orgone Energy. It is fighting fire with fire and that is why we are going to win. We are dealing with the knowledge of the future." He patted my shoulder. "And you, Peeps, may be the first of that generation of children of the future. Here at the age of eleven you have already disabled a flying saucer using cosmic Orgone Energy. Quite a feat."

I was proud and happy as we walked back and stayed outside with Bill while Daddy went inside to get Eva. We stood there for a minute or two looking at the sky and then Bill said, "You did a real good job, Peter. You really are a pretty good soldier. In fact—" he grinned—"I guess that after tonight, you'd better change those sergeants' stripes to lieutenants' bars. I think you've earned it."

I was so happy I didn't know what to say. Bill smiled at me as if he knew how happy I was. When Eva came out and they got in the car, he leaned out of the window as the car started down the drive.

"Goodnight, Lieutenant," he said. We saluted.

It felt good. I was proud and happy. I had disabled a flying saucer and was in the Cosmic Engineers. And it was okay if a battle came with the spaceships or even the government because I was going to be a brave soldier and I had just gotten a promotion.

I wished Toreano were there to see me.

Inside, Daddy was at his desk, writing in his big red notebook. His pen scratched loudly. The record player was playing Beethoven's Ninth Symphony. I sat down on the couch and listened for a while.

"I feel a lot better after Orurizing," I said.

"Ja," said Daddy.

I sat back on the couch and let the music pick me up and carry me.

"Daddy, remember we talked about getting uniforms?"

"Yes."

"Well, I think we ought to get blue ones. And maybe they could have white belts like they have on road patrol." If I had brought my belt home I could have worn it on the cloudbuster.

Daddy was humming and nodding with the music. He looked at me and then he looked up.

"Ja. And a nice flag, too. I think a blue flag with the spinning wave emblazoned in white. For the sky and the stars."

"I like green too. Maybe we could make it green and blue. Green for the grass we're going to make."

I closed my eyes and my mind was joined with Daddy's and

Beethoven's and we were all seeing the same thing: a great plain with bold white clouds climbing the sky like mighty stallions, and coming through the clouds on beams of sunlight was the Army of Cosmic Engineers marching straight, forward, and proud beneath tall flags snapping in the wind, marching proudly in smart blue uniforms with hats with shiny brims and shiny white belts. First Daddy—the General—and then Bill and Eva and me, and Tom and the others, maybe even Ray could be one of us and we would march onward to victory over the EAs and the FDA.

"And silk, so it would wave nicely in the wind."

"Our wind."

"Ja, sonny, our wind."

Chapter 2

Judge me, O God, and plead my cause against an ungodly nation: O deliver me from the deceitful and unjust man. For thou art the God of my strength: Why dost thou cast me off? Why go I mourning because of the oppression of the enemy?

O send out thy light and thy truth: let them lead me; let them bring me unto thy holy hill, and to thy tabernacles.

43rd Psalm

Monsieur?

Breathing woke me up slowly. Everything else was numb except this tingling where the breathing came in and out, louder and louder. Then there was another person breathing too and I tried to remember what was familiar because something had already happened that I didn't remember again.

"*Monsieur? Monsieur?*" I shook my head. The voice tumbled out of the breathing. "*Monsieur?*" When I opened my eyes the doctor was looking at me, talking to me in French in a French hospital . . . but there was another hospital, from the dream. . . .

The doctor told me that they had not succeeded in getting my shoulder back in its socket. He said they would have to give me gas again and I was frightened because that other dream in another hospital was almost there in my mind. It was something about the shoulder or the arm, the same arm. The doctor said it was a very bad dislocation.

"*Une luxation très sévère,*" he said.

"Ipswich," I said.

"*Comment?*"

I shook my head. The doctor smiled and said they would have to give me gas again but the hospital was almost there. It was in Ipswich. The nurse was getting the mask ready but I couldn't remember. The hospital's crazy darkness flitted against my head. I've got to remember what it was in that dream because there was *another* dream. The nurse brought the mask close to my face. It was a crazy summer in England. I raced old rickety bicycles all summer up and down the paths of a huge old mental hospital, dodging patients on the paths. Everybody said I was going to crash. . . .

"*Attendez!*" I shouted. The doctor and nurse looked astonished. It was after I lived in Arizona. I left Arizona and went to live with my mother. In the summer of 1956 she wanted to take me to England to see her relatives but I wasn't sure I wanted to go. I wanted to stay with my father because something bad was going to happen, but I ended up going. It was a miserable summer. I spent my time being miserable and breaking things. I broke, by accident, a large quantity of my aunt's fine china. On a trip to Scotland I broke, by accident, my eyeglasses, and spent the entire trip sulking beneath a raincoat. Finally, shortly before we returned to America where I was to spend the rest of the summer with my father at Orgonon, we spent a few days in Ipswich, where my uncle worked as a resident psychiatrist in a mental hospital. Riding a bicycle across the insane asylum grounds like a maniac, I broke, by accident, my right arm. When they took me to the hospital, they gave me gas.

THERE WAS ANOTHER DREAM!

"The dream!" I shouted. I sat up and looked at the doctor and nurses. They looked bewildered. "I gotta find that dream!" I shouted. "I'm gonna get it!"

In broken French I explained to the doctor that I would give him a signal with my hand when to start working on the shoulder. I needed time to get into the gas, into the dream, and really get knocked out. I told the doctor not to start until I gave him the signal. He shrugged and the others nodded.

"Okay, *allons-y*," I said.

The nurse brought the mask up slowly and I raised my left hand, forefinger extended. I had to remember everything, absolutely everything that happened that summer after I broke my arm. The mask was snug against my face. The hissing began and I breathed deeply, sucking the gas to get the dream. Heavy, soft, and full, filling me like an enormous breast, it came steadily, and through the hissing I remembered the huge hospital spreading out around me. Stop! Wait! This is scary! This is a mental hospital! I tried to shout but already the rainy brick dark English hospital was so heavy it melted my mouth and it began to breathe too, and grew bigger and bigger, expanding like a great balloon filling me and it was going to burst. All the bricks were going to tumble over me, overtaking and drowning me like the grey ocean of numb needles when I was a baby boy in Maine wearing blue pajamas with a tiny tiny black dot that got bigger and bigger and bigger and was all black.

Streams of water went like rivers through the white hair on Daddy's chest and made his cloudy white hair come down around his face so it was holding up his cheeks as he smiled.

I smiled back and turned around underneath the shower, letting it pour right on top of my head and then drip all over me.

Standing in the cool water in the sun on the observatory roof we could see all the way to Mount Washington and all across

Orgonon past the lake and past Burnham Hill way up to Saddleback. I liked the rooftop shower.

I was happy to be back at Orgonon after an awful summer in England. It made me feel good to stand on the observatory roof and see it again. The big field in front of the observatory was full of waving grass all the way to the bottom. When I was younger the trees were lower and you could see the laboratory roof at the bottom of the hill but now you just have to know it is there because the road up to it from the Badger Road is there. Badger Road runs through the fields of Orgonon down to the main road. But before the main road is the turnoff to our cabin, the lower cabin with a red roof, but you can only barely see it because the trees have gotten older around it too, and made the path from the cabin to the lake darker.

Orgonon is so big that if I stretch my arms out in the sunlight, everything that is inside my arms from the observatory to the lake is ours.

After Daddy turned off the shower, it was quiet except for water dripping through the wet boards onto the gravel roof and, in the trees, birds. The gravel hurt my feet a little as I walked to the edge of the roof. It wasn't like when I was younger and went barefoot and had tough feet.

"Be careful at the edge," said Daddy.

"I will. I just wanted to get a better look at the field. Look how blue the lake is. There is a lot of Orgone today." I was getting pretty good at observing.

"Yes, it is very charged." He wiped himself off with a big bath towel except for where his baggy underpants dripped. He never went naked. But I did all the time and all over me shiny drops of water sparkled in the sun like golden medals.

Looking down into the fields I could see Toreano leading the troops on maneuvers. Ever since I got back from England, we'd been getting ready. Daddy said the agents might come any day.

"Daddy, can we shoot?" The cast had only been off for a few days and I wanted to make sure I could still shoot straight. The accumulator helped my arm get better fast so my arm felt pretty strong.

"Yes, if you would like to."

"Can I shoot the .45?"

"No, you shoot your rifle. I'll use the .45."

"When will I be able to use the .45?"

"You will be able to use it soon."

We went downstairs to get dressed and then I went into the little room next to the study where Daddy kept the guns. My rifle was a Winchester carbine .32–.20 and its serial number was 906608. It was patented in 1864 and James Stewart had one like it in the movie where his saddle had a bell, only his had a ring on the side. At first I just had a BB gun and once when I was playing with it over at Tom's I pulled the cock lever open and pulled the trigger. The lever shot back and cut my finger almost off. There was a lot of blood but the accumulator healed it fast but I think I got a nerve because whenever I hit the finger against something it buzzes inside. Then when I was about seven or eight Daddy got me a .22 special. It was a nice gun but it backfired. So before we went to Tucson we went to Pearson's in Farmington and got the .32–.20.

I kept it in the rack with Daddy's other guns. He had a double-barrel 12-gauge shotgun with a .38–.55 Winchester underneath it that I could hardly lift, a Mannlicher and a Mauser. They were 8- or 9-millimeter guns that I couldn't shoot yet. Then there was a .32 special that he gave to Bill just in case, and hanging in the holster, the .45.

Daddy had dressed in his khaki pants and was waiting for me on the porch, looking through binoculars checking out the atmosphere.

"Go ahead," he said.

I put three shells in the magazine and walked up to the edge of the railing. Daddy stood back by the big window. We're always careful. Daddy told me never to point a gun at anyone because it is not good.

The sound of the metal sliding around the chamber and the bullet slipping in was just like a western. *Click* I brought the lever up and brought the sights into line over the target just like Daddy had showed me with his fingers so that the pointer at the end of the barrel came right into the V. He showed me with his fingers. It was like at school one day a girl made a V with her fingers and poked another finger into the V. What does it mean? she said. I said I didn't know and she said it was fuck.

Bang!

In comics the guns go *krang*. They go *pow pow* or *krang*. Once I saw a war comic and the guns went *budda budda budda* and *wham*. My rifle was actually more like *krang*.

"Very good," said Daddy, lowering his binoculars. "Almost bullseye. Try again." From Saddleback the echo came back like the sound of a lot of rain falling all at once.

I turned back to the railing and cocked the rifle. The spent shell fell on the gravel. The target came in front of the sights. Fuck was bad because it was without love. War wasn't love either but it was okay against the communists.

Krang!

The wooden block shook. Daddy focused the binoculars. "Nah, this time you were a bit off. Do you have another?"

I nodded. The echo fell.

"Okay, try again."

Open, shut, *click*, aim. And the people out to get Daddy.
Krang!

"Ja. Good. It was closer than the first, but still not bullseye. Now I shall shoot."

In my echo from Saddleback, Daddy took the .45 out of his holster and handed me the glasses.

He went up to the railing and pulled the magazine out to check it. He knocked it back in with the palm of his hand, pulled the top of the gun back to cock it, and aimed. As soon as his arm was held out straight I started to wince because the .45 was a lot louder than the .32–.20. My eyes kept closing all by themselves and my shoulder went up.

Boom!

I felt the noise and saw Daddy's hand fly up in the air with the kick. The .32–.20 hardly kicked at all but the .45 kicked hard. In westerns they never show guns kicking but when you shoot a real gun it kicks hard and that is why Daddy's other guns had shoulder pads.

The echo came back across the lake as I raised the binoculars.

The target filled up almost the whole lens, making it look close and grainy. There was a big hole right in the middle and three smaller holes near it.

"You got bullseye!"

Scattered around the wood block in the grainy lens were chips of wood from where other bullets had hit and farther back in the woods was an overgrown place with baby blueberry bushes growing where Tom and I burned brush together a long time ago in winter.

I turned the binoculars around and looked at Daddy through the big end. He looked very far away. He was aiming again, getting ready to shoot. Maybe looking this way will make the sound smaller too.

Boom!

He turned and looked at me.

"What are you doing?"

"I just turned the binoculars around. It made you look smaller." The echo passed us like heavy water. "Daddy, will I be able to stay with you when the battle is over?"

"I hope so, Peter. I hope when it is over we will be able to live together and be happy with Aurora."

Daddy's new girl friend was Aurora. I didn't know if I liked her or not. She lived in Washington, D.C., and Daddy wanted me to like her a lot. He talked about her for a while and then he talked about the appeal.

"We shall know soon if I will have to go to jail or not. I hope the appeal will be accepted, because I think the trial made it clear what we stand for. Peter, there is a real conspiracy against my work. Somewhere, someone does not want this work in Orgonomy to continue. I do not know why, although I am beginning to understand. You must understand that I might die. Someone might try to kill me."

He stopped and looked at me. "Peeps, please don't run away."

Everyone ran away. At the trial they all sent me a telegram saying hello. In the telegram they called me a lieutenant. I wanted to go to the trial but I had to go to school. There was a trial because everyone is afraid of Orgone Energy and they said that Daddy couldn't let people use accumulators any more but he did and so they are going to do something bad. I will be brave.

"Whatever happens, I want you to be brave and to live your own life. That is why it is good for you to be with Mummy now and go to the boarding school. It is important for you to have friends and grow up where there isn't so much tension. You must live your own life. And whatever happens to me, you must always be brave."

The binoculars pressed between us I held him so tightly. I wanted to cry but there was not time. We had to be ready.

"I understand," I said, "and I'll be brave."

I gave him my eyes and we smiled. He went inside to do some work.

I stood on the railing alone for a while and looked at Orgonon through the glasses. Toreano was leading a troop through the woods and waved. I was proud to be guarding Orgonon.

After I cleaned the guns I went through the study where Daddy was working and went up the stairs to the roof.

The little room on the roof of the observatory was a little lab. A pendulum hung from the ceiling and I made it swing slowly. By the door to the roof I touched the knob on the oscilloscope that makes the snake wiggle. Sometimes Daddy let me play with the knobs and make the snake into a dot and the dot into a line.

Through the window, drops of water sparkled on the damp boards under the outdoor shower. I held the binoculars up and focused them down so that the wet shower boards were all out of focus and sparkled fuzzily in different colors. No-focus was like a prism that broke up the sparkles so that each drop of water had red, blue, and yellow sparklers against the dull brown boards.

I lifted the binoculars and looked at the horizon, all a fuzzy blur of sky and mountains. Below the fuzzy line the fuzzy red roof of the lower cabin was bright in the middle of green blobs of trees and the road was blurry with a funny moving sparkle on it. I turned the focus knob and the moving sparkle settled on the road and became sharper and sharper until it was a shiny black car rolling quietly along the road with a government seal on the side.

"Daddy! Daddy!" I screamed, running down the stairs, "Daddy! They're here! They're coming! The agents are here!"

Daddy got up from his desk and walked quickly out onto the porch and I ran after him. His face was very stern.

"Give me the glasses."

He focused quickly down to the road by the lab where the black car had stopped in the driveway. I held my breath until my heart pounded all the way up into my head.

"Who is it, Daddy? Are they coming to get you?"

I was so afraid. Daddy always said they would have to take him away in chains.

"I don't know. Wait."

He stood very still, holding the binoculars with both hands. The black car was standing still in the driveway. The Mannlicher had a telescopic sight too, so we could get them from here.

"What are they doing?"

"I don't know. Just sitting there."

Daddy could probably see their faces through the glasses. All I could see was the car. I only shot once with a telescopic sight but it is easy with the crosshairs.

The car started to move up the road a bit and then it stopped just about where the sign says BY APPOINTMENT ONLY. Then it rolled back toward the turnoff, glinting all the time in the sun. It turned around and started down the road away from Orgonon toward town. The binoculars followed the car until it was out of sight.

"Ahem. AHEM ahem. Well, perhaps they will call for once." He turned and walked back toward the study.

"Do you think they will come back?"

"Yes, but I think this time they will call. I think we made the message quite clear the last time."

For a long time Daddy and Bill carried guns around in their cars because agents were coming up all the time and not even calling or asking for an appointment, just coming right up. That made Daddy mad. And people were shooting holes in our Orgonon sign. That made Daddy really mad. That was when he told me he wanted me to start wearing a whistle. He gave me a shiny metal police whistle on a piece of rawhide to wear around my neck when I played out in the fields. If anyone tried to get me I was supposed to whistle.

He sat down at his desk and cranked the telephone, waiting for the operator ahem ahem.

"Yes, operator. Would you please get me six four ring three?"

While he waited for the operator to get the number, he put on his glasses and shifted some papers on his desk. Then he looked over his glasses at me.

"Wait a moment. Don't go away. Ja. Moise!"

He waved a finger at me for me to sit down. I sat in one of the big soft grey chairs next to the fireplace and put my finger in one of the funny soft places that went back and forth in the material. It went back and forth with my finger.

"Moise. This is Dr. Reich speaking. Ja. We have just seen a car stop at the gate and I think it is Food and Drug Administration people again. I looked with the glasses and I think I saw a U.S. marshal too. Ja. About the accumulators."

Bill's voice sounded all high and squiggly coming across the room but I couldn't hear what he was saying.

"Ja. They drove away without coming up and I think they will probably telephone before they come back. I think we made our point. I wonder if you could come over right away. Ja. Good."

Bill's voice squiggled out again. Daddy looked at his watch.

"No. Ja. Mr. Ross will be back from lunch soon too. Okay. See you. Goodbye."

After he hung up he put some papers away and opened up one of his red books. His pen scratched for a few minutes and the material in the chair wiggled against my finger. The clock ticked.

"Daddy?"

"Ja?"

"What is going to happen?"

"Are you scared?"

"I guess a little bit. I don't want them to hurt you."

"Come here."

He moved his chair away from his desk and held his arms out to me. I ran across the carpet to Daddy.

He put his hands on my shoulders and looked at me deeply.

"Look at me, Peeps." He looked worried and sad and I could feel his warmth and the smell of oil on his skin. He used baby oil for his skin disease and sometimes he smelled like a baby. His eyes were so good to me it always made me want to cry.

"Peeps, you are a very good soldier and you are very strong. But you must be stronger. We are fighting a very tough battle against the anti-life forces. It is very hard sometimes. Many people ran away. You have been very brave."

I nodded. It was too much for everybody. Oranur, the flying saucers, the cloudbuster, and the FDA. A lot of people thought Daddy was crazy. There were spies who stole the Orgone motor. And everyone who ran away, except me and Bill and Eva, was afraid of truth. We had truth.

"You know, Peeps, hundreds of years ago there was a sickness called the black plague. It went all over Europe killing thousands and thousands of people. Many good doctors worked very hard to cure the people but very often they died too, victims of the plague. Today, I have discovered a new kind of plague.

"It is an emotional plague that comes from within. It kills people emotionally and makes them keep their belly tight. It makes them lie and slander and spy. This emotional plague is more vicious than the black plague because the people do not want to be cured. They strike out in rage at one who tries to cure it because they have been sick so long they think the sickness is health. And that is why they are attacking me. I am trying to tell them that they don't have to hate and they hate me for it. We have discussed this many times, do you remember?"

I nodded and held onto his eyes because I could not let go.

"The hate and the attacks started many years ago when I was forced to leave Germany, Austria, Denmark, and Norway. For years people who were afraid of what I said have spread rumors that I was insane. Here in America I have been barred from professional organizations and, as you know, attacked by the government. You know they have orders to burn some of my books this week.

"I can't believe this is happening, but it is. Strange things have happened before: the Orgone motor being stolen, the Einstein affair, the Air Force . . . it all adds up to an incredible conspiracy. And it is frightening. Of course it is frightening. They do not look at the work, they attack me personally. Peeps, people do not fight back like this unless they are themselves frightened and they are frightened by the truth of cosmic Orgone Energy. They are frightened by life.

"But Peeps, no matter what happens, I will not stop my work. No matter what happens the work must go on. Nothing can stop the truth. No laws can stop scientific research. That is why we are fighting, and that is why I may have to die. Truth is deadly and they know I am right. The emotional plague can kill.

"I told them that in court, and they refused to listen. I told them that a court of law could not judge basic scientific principles and they refused to look at the real issues. It doesn't matter that they found me guilty, because even if we lose the appeal we have really won. That is why this is such an important battle and why you must be very brave. It is very hard to stand up for truth but it is very important. That is why I always told you never to lie.

"Now listen. The men may come back and I want you to be a brave soldier and help. Will you be strong?"

"Yup."

"All right. I want you to go to the lab. When Moise comes, tell him to come directly up here and when Mr. Ross comes back from lunch tell him I want him to come up here also. If the FDA men come back, I want you to stop the car at the lab and telephone me to see if I shall come down or if they will come up. Don't let them come up without first telephoning. Okay?"

"Okay." I started to go, but he held me.

"Peeps?"

"What?"

"Give me your eyes."

As I walked around the front of the observatory and started down the hill, I heard the telephone ring.

I didn't know what was going to happen but I wasn't scared. Toreano came up and brought me a pony. We rode down the hill together.

Daddy was so serious and worried. I know there are a lot of bad things people say about him. One day a long time ago when I was at the observatory, I found a whole stack of magazines in the basement. They had pictures of lots of girls with their breasts almost showing and movie stars. One of them was *Uncensored*. I started looking through one of the magazines because it was exciting to see the soft curvy breasts and legs. There were pretty girls struggling with tough guys with crew cuts and swastikas. But that was fucking.

Then there was a picture of a naked girl jiggling her breasts in front of a row of accumulators. There were men staring out of the accumulators at the girl and the story said that the men were masturbating and that the accumulator—only they called it an Orgone box—was supposed to give them huge orgasms.

I haven't masturbated yet but when I do it will feel good. And it doesn't matter if people say it is bad because they are sick. Daddy said I could use Vaseline or oil to rub my penis. I told him I didn't understand but he said just wait.

Then there was another magazine that didn't have as many pictures but there was a long story about how we had machine-gun guards around Orgonon and lots of naked people running around inside protected by barbed-wire fences. But I'm the only person I know who ran around naked a lot. It scared me that people thought that.

Besides, I've used an accumulator and it makes me feel better.

Mummy used it when she burned her hand and it healed much faster than usual. The one Daddy uses has a light in it so you can read and there is one with a board in it for your chest, too.

I like it because it makes you tingly and warm and that is when it is time to come out. Like when I cut my finger with the BB gun, Daddy put the shooter on it and said wait until it starts to tingle and then take it off. The tingling meant it was alive and moving.

I used the funnel on my hand when I pushed my hand through the washing-machine wringer, too. I was helping Mummy put laundry through the ringer and for a long time I just stared at the clothes going in between the two white wringers and coming out on the other side all smooth and flat.

So I watched the wet lumpy clothes go in one side and smooth out the other and then all of a sudden I just put my hand up after a pillow case and it started to go through the ringer. Mummy screamed when she saw my fingers come out the other side and before my hand got all the way through she reached up and hit the release bar and the rollers came apart. She took my hand in hers and we went out onto the porch where Daddy was reading. Why did you do it? they asked. I said I didn't know. Daddy got kind of mad, but he just went and got the Orgone funnel and put it over my hand. In a few minutes it started tingling and feeling better.

Daddy always said staring is a sign of sickness.

When we got to the lab I told Toreano to go out and get the troops ready. He rode off and I got the key out of the hiding place and opened the lab.

As soon as I opened the door, the cool dry chemical smell rushed outside. It was cooler inside and behind the chemical smell was the headachy smell of Oranur. The lab hadn't changed hardly at all since Oranur because it still had a high charge and couldn't be used. No one had used it for nearly four years.

Most of the scientific stuff had been moved to the observatory, so all that was left were a few tables and chairs and cabinets and empty jars and boxes and the smell. Standing near the door were several accumulators that were sent back by people who were afraid to use them because of the FDA. The FDA made people afraid.

It was very quiet and there were no cars coming so I poked around in the little back rooms. Paint was peeling off the hot-water heater in the bathroom and the floor creaked. The next room was where there were lots of samples of rocks and wood that were decayed by DOR. Almost all the shelves had old samples in jars and rocks with faded pieces of paper with dates and places. Up on one shelf were bottles of stuff and one of them had a yellowish puffy mass of stuff floating in clear liquid.

Once, when there were people here, a lady came in this room with me and showed me the bottle. She said it was a tumor and then she unbuttoned her blouse. Her skin was pretty with soft yellow light from the window coming through the cloth onto her soft breast, making it look soft and the nipple all dark and then she lifted the other side of her blouse where there were lots of Band-aids where the other breast was supposed to be. She said it was the tumor in the jar and I tried to be serious but I was scared.

Beep! Beep!

Tom had stopped the pickup in front of the lab and was leaning out of the window. I ran outside.

"Hi, Tom."

"Hi, Pete. I seen the lab door was open and wondered if that was you."

He sat back as I ran up to the window. His hand shook on the gear shift. "What you doin' down here all by yourself?"

"Tom, some agents came just before and then they went away. Daddy said you're supposed to go right up to the observatory."

Tom looked up the road and started to shift into first. Then he turned and looked back at me.

"What about you? Are you stayin' here?"

"Yes. Bill is supposed to come too and I have to tell him to go up to the hill too. And then if the agents come back I'm supposed to stop them here and call on the phone."

The gear-shift lever fell into first under Tom's hand.

"Okay. Now you be careful."

"Okay, Tom."

He let the clutch out and started up the hill. I walked into the road and watched the tailgate disappear up the first little hill in the woods and walked the rest of the way across the road in between the barn and the tractor shed to the hard mossy dirt behind. My penis was white in my hand as I spread my legs to pee. The foreskin was closed all the way down and when the pee came out it had to find a way out in a ripply yellow line into the dirt. I might have been peeing on Experiment 20. They buried it here years ago, maybe to let it be near the earth or something. Experiment 20—I used to call it X X—was very important. For a long time, when people were still here they stood next to the big busy tables in the lab with microscopes, holding glass bottles up in the air. Everybody talked about the experiment for a long time and then one day they all walked out here and planted it, in their white coats standing in the woods. I watched it from my treehouse.

I shook off the last drops, put it back, and went out across the grass to the cloudbuster platform near the lab. We had lots of cloudbusters, some on trucks and some on platforms. One was at the lab and there were two up at the observatory. That way, we could make big operations with a lot of them. Like an army.

Up on the platform was an equipment box that Tom built. He built a lot of things. Inside it were some rocks and a folded piece of paper. It was an old map I had made showing how to make rain:

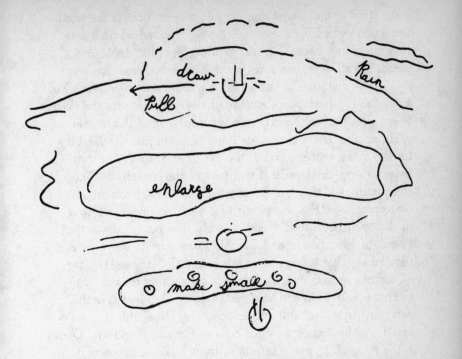

When there is a big drawing we use more than one cloudbuster
and have a special system to tell which direction to draw from,
since the cloudbusters are far apart. We worked it out with
whistles. My metal whistle with the rawhide necklace is the
loudest so I usually stay with Daddy and relay his commands.
One blast is north; three long blasts means west. Four is south
because we don't use it very often, and three short ones means
east. Two is Zenith. Zenith means pipes straight up in the air
but it sounds like God or a place in California. It is like a
gathering place. After drawing for a few minutes, Zenith is like
pulling in the drawstring on my striped marble bag and holding
the sky together. Once it is in the bag you can loosen it up
again and do things with wind and clouds and energy.

Sometimes we punch holes in the clouds and sometimes we
bring clouds together. Sometimes when it is a bad day we

make it move and sometimes we just play and catch the wind. Once there was a big hurricane coming. The radio said it was very dangerous because it was heading right for the Maine coast. We all went out and operated and the hurricane went away. The man on the radio said it was very strange how all of a sudden the hurricane just started swerving out into the ocean. We were all proud. Daddy said we were men of the future.

He wrote a letter to the Air Force about it just like he did for the flying saucers, and to the Weather Bureau. But they never answered. He said it was part of the conspiracy. The conspiracy was that the Communists and Hoodlums in Government—HIGs—were out to get us but they can't do it in the open because they are weasels. The conspiracy is that President Eisenhower and the Air Force are on our side and they know what is happening but can't help. Or else they are all against us and that is why they are coming today.

That is why I have to be a good soldier. Daddy was in the Austrian Army and Bill was in the Navy. Now Bill is a major and I'm a lieutenant in the Corps of Cosmic Engineers. Daddy is the general. In my other outfit, though, I'm Lieutenant Cohill from *She Wore a Yellow Ribbon*.

Toreano rode up with a dispatch that Bill was coming, so I went back to the lab and waited. His green station wagon came up the road. He turned up the drive and when he got close I stood at attention and saluted. He leaned over to the window as he drove past and threw a salute back at me.

"Good luck, Lieutenant!"

"Yes, sir!"

Before going back into the lab I jumped off the porch and went out into the grass. I faced the forest and saluted.

"All right, men, this is going to be a tough job." The officers and sergeants sat tall in their saddles, a straight line in front of the trees. Dry poplar leaves clattered overhead and the breeze made their yellow scarves wave too. "I want you all to be brave and carry on like good soldiers. I don't know what is going to happen today but I want you to be ready at all times. We can't let the general down. Take your posts. Dismissed."

Back inside the lab I walked all the way to the end of the big room to the telephone and looked out of the window. It was all quiet except for the loud cricket that buzzes sometimes. Actually the cricket was an Indian scout. Crows cawed in the trees.

On the table next to the telephone all covered with dust was an old army-green telescope. I used to play with it all the time when the lab was open because it had a dial on top that changed the picture into different colors. Daddy used it to watch Orgone Energy streaming across the fields. I looked down into it and it turned Orgonon into a neat rectangle like a sharp new postcard at the drugstore. The road came out of the trees in the upper right-hand corner above the apple orchard. It ran across the picture, under the red lower cabin roof and across the turnoff to the lab. *Click.* It was yellow, bright yellow as if the sun came down and lay over everything. *Click* all green and dark like a dreamnight. *Click* bright red like a red fire on the trees, the road, even our already red roof. *Click.* Natural. So real and sharp it is just like a new postcard with green grass and blue sky and dark mountains, nothing moving except the black car coming out of the upper corner and moving slowly down the road throwing sparks of light at me from the roof.

I couldn't breathe. The dial clicked slowly through red yellow green. Each time there was a black place before the new color making the car stop for a second. I turned faster and faster because if I turned the dial fast enough it would stop the car and send it backward blue into the yellow grass and red forest.

But the car was shiny black and slowed down in front of the lab in a green field of red dust.

Dust was still settling on the shiny black hood as I came out the door squinting in the sunlight. There were three men in the car. Two in front and one in back. They wore shiny thin neckties and white shirts and dark suits. Their faces were shiny and their eyes weren't good. The man next to the driver leaned out the window. He stretched his hand out to me. In it was a little black leather wallet with a shiny badge in it. The man said he was a United States marshal. .

"These other men are Food and Drug Administration agents. We'd like to see Dr. Reich."

I looked into the window. Holding my teeth together made me braver and look more like Gary Cooper or somebody. The agents didn't move. The one in the back nodded. I straightened up and looked at the marshal. His suit was lumpy. Maybe he had a gun next to his armpit. It would smell bad. I just kept looking at the men without answering. Finally the marshal said, "Uh, we called."

"Okay. But you'll have to wait until I go in and call. It's by appointment only, you know."

"Yes. Well, uh, like I say, we called. I think the doctor is expecting us."

"Well, I still have to call to tell him you are here. It will just take a minute."

The marshal nodded.

Trying not to run, I turned and went back into the lab. I had to be calm and slow. My hand touched every nail in the aluminum molding on every table as I walked through the lab to the telephone, looking back to watch the black car. And brave. The sun was a yellow dot on the black car trunk. The men were talking. One of them turned around and looked out of the window at the lab.

I held the receiver down with one hand and cranked with the other. Two longs and a short. Two longs and a short. Then I picked up the receiver. It shook, so I squeezed it harder. Daddy picked up in the observatory.

"Ja. Pete?"

"Daddy. They're here. One is a U.S. marshal and the two others are—"

"Ja. I know. Now tell them—"

Outside, the sun started to slip off the trunk of the black car. The car was rolling. It couldn't be rolling uphill. Daddy's voice squiggled and the sun dropped all the way off the car into swirls of dust and tears.

"Daddy! They didn't wait!"

Tears tangled my words making the receiver wet and shiny. The car disappeared around the side of the lab up the hill.

"Daddy! They're coming up! OH DADDY OH GOD THEY DIDN'T WAIT. THEY'RE COMING UP DADDY THEY'RE COMING UP!"

The screen door slammed before the receiver hit the floor. Grass was already whipping my legs as I ran up the hill. The whole field was swimming and I cried *uunh* each time I breathed out and it made it easier to run uphill.

Everett Quimby said if you run with your hands open you could go faster so my hands were wide open going back and forth like a train all the way up the hill like a train running. Because if I ran fast enough maybe I could beat them to the top of the hill and warn Daddy. What did they want? What did they want? Why did they always make us unhappy? If I just watched my palms running back and forth *uunnh* like a train it would go faster than if I kept watching the top of the hill for the observatory to start coming out. The hands went faster and then they went slower with *unhs*. I walked for a minute almost at the top. Stopped. There was no sound of cars and you could always tell just where a car was on the hill by the noise it made climbing and going around corners.

Uuunh I started to run again and when I got to the top all I heard was my breathing, salt at the corners of my mouth. I ran up the side of the porch and across the front. The black car was parked in the lot with the pickup and Bill's car. Daddy's car was in the garage. Up the last thin steps to the door I ran and then tried to stop the hard breathing and *uunhs* to listen.

There was no noise. If they had guns . . . With silencers I wouldn't have heard any shots.

Quietly on the red rug on the steps I went upstairs listening at the first landing and then going all the way to the top, looking into the study. Daddy was sitting at his desk. The three men were standing in front of the desk with their backs to me. Tom and Bill were by the window. Daddy had on his red-and-black checkered shirt and his pens were shiny in the pocket next to his heart.

I hid behind the double doors right underneath the photograph of two hands and the energy field. You can feel Orgone if you hold your palms apart and make them go in and out. I sniffed and wiped my nose.

Daddy looked in between the men and saw me. He nodded and motioned for me to come. I ran across the carpet to Daddy.

The men turned to look as I ran past them and stood next to Daddy behind the desk. The men's ties were shiny and their mouths moved but it didn't look like their mouths were saying the same words I heard.

"That's just what we were told to do, Doctor. . . . Uh, you sure you want the boy here?"

My back stiffened and I bit my lower lip to stop it from moving.

"Yes. That is all right. Go ahead," said Daddy. I put my hand on the back of his chair.

The man talking was the marshal. His hair was short and close to his head. The corners of his jaw stuck out close to his ears. The other two men looked at him and then at Daddy with their hands behind their backs.

"Well, Doctor, the orders say that it is supposed to be done today, right here at Orgy-non. I'm sorry, Doctor."

"Well, don't be sorry. We must all follow our orders, right?"

The marshal tried to smile. "Yup, that's right, Doctor."

"So. How is it to be done?" Daddy had a pencil in his hand. He hit the eraser against the table and slid his forefinger and thumb down the pencil, grabbed the eraser, flipped the pencil over and hit the point of the pencil against the table. *Tic.* Then he slid his fingers down to the point and did it again. *Toc.* He did it again and again. "Shall we use our bare hands?"

He smiled and turned to Tom and Bill. Bill laughed and nodded. Tom smiled and shuffled his feet. The two men cleared their throats and watched the pencil go up and down.

"Well, Doctor, I'm sure we can find something. You must have hammers, picks, saws, axes. . . ."

I could feel the glow from Daddy's head. Around his ears it was redder and I knew he was looking at them very hard because one by one their eyes dropped and they shuffled their feet. The pencil went up and down making a soft noise on the desk. Nobody said a word. The marshal looked back and tried to smile but then the smile went away and he watched the pencil. Daddy was warm. He smelled like a baby. His red shirt moved with his breathing as he looked at the men.

Sometimes he showed me the way crazy people look. He would suddenly stop and let his face sag and his eyes get dim. His eyes would look off and I would stand in front of them and wave but he wouldn't even blink. It was scary and I always yelled stop Daddy stop. Then when he stopped he smiled and said that that is a sign people have gone crazy when their eyes are dim and don't move. That is why we always do eye exercises. When he is angry his face drops and his eyes drill into you. His whole face gets red and his eyes burn and make you hot like a fire. He said the only color painters can't paint is the color of a dying fire.

The pencil went *toc* against the desk and the clock over the fireplace went *tic* and sometimes they went *tic* together *toc*. Finally after a long time Daddy said, "Mr. Ross, take Peter and go to the lab. Start dismantling the accumulators. Get some

53

axes out." The pencil stopped but his eyes didn't move. The men still watched the pencil.

Tom nodded. "Okay, Doctor." He looked at me and nodded to the door. Daddy turned to me. His eyes said be brave.

The side of the truck was hot against my arm but I could bear it.

When we got to the lab we parked the truck and went into the barn.

"You know where the screwdrivers are, Pete. Why don't you get a couple?"

He pulled shiny two-bladed axes off the wall while I went to the tool box and got some screwdrivers with clear yellow handles. I got my red-handled screwdriver out of my toolbox and stuck them all in my back pocket and followed Tom out the door.

Tom spread three axes out on the tailgate of the pickup. They glinted. The blade on my ax was smaller because we used it to cut brush in winter and it had been sharpened so much that the blade just got littler and littler. The handle had tape around it at the top because once when I was learning how to swing it I hit the handle against the tree instead of the blade and it shivered all the way down like when you hit a baseball with the thin part of the bat. Tom put black tape around the top part so it was okay.

There is a special way to swing an ax that Tom taught me and on this ax it was even easier because Tom said he used my ax for years and years before he gave it to me and the handle was darker and smoother than the other axes and it smelled good.

Tom looked at me from the lab porch.

"Let's go," he said.

He put a tall glass jar on one of the tables and started unscrewing, dropping the screws into the jar.

Tom could unscrew faster than I could. He just flipped his wrist and they came out. I had to turn a lot harder but I could still do it pretty good.

Screws clinked in the jar. Tom already had the door and a side off one accumulator. He leaned them against the wall.

Car noises came through the window. First Daddy's car and then the agent's and Bill's. They all got out and walked to the lab. All their shadows made the doorway darker.

Bill came over, pulled a screwdriver out of my back pocket, and helped unscrew. The hardest part was reaching the high hinges, especially if you wanted to watch the men at the same time. I wished I had hidden my gun in case they tried something. The hinges were like silver butterflies holding onto the pale yellow corners of the accumulator. After the screws came out they fluttered into my hand and when I had a whole bunch I took them over to the jar. Everyone was so quiet I was scared.

The three men were standing by the green telescope looking out of the windows. One of them was writing in a black book. Daddy was walking around checking boxes and watching us. Tom looked at him.

"Doctor, where do you want us to take them?"

The men looked up.

Daddy said, "Well, gentlemen, do your orders say anything about where to do it?"

"Uh, no, Doctor."

"So." Daddy walked out onto the porch and looked out across the meadow toward the cloudbuster. Then he turned and looked the other way into the sun. The road forked. The tar part went up the hill and turned right toward the observatory. The other part was the tractor road that Tom uses to get to the back field. I like mowing with Tom except once I fell off. The sun was shining on the grassy place where the two roads made a V. "Ahem. AHEM ahem. Mr. Ross?"

"Yes, Doctor." Tom went onto the porch dropping a handful

of screws into the jar along the way. The jar was almost full. They stood on the porch for a minute then Daddy pointed to the hospital field and they came back in.

Tom said, "Come on, Pete."

He grabbed the side of an accumulator and started out the door. I grabbed a top and followed him. Bill stayed in the lab watching the men. We walked up the road lugging the pieces and then crossed onto the grass where tractor tires had worn the grass away. Tom walked down the tractor road a ways and then off into the little clearing between the two roads. He set his piece down in the middle of the V between the road to the observatory and the road to the fields. I laid my top on top. On the way back we passed Bill carrying more sides. Daddy was on the porch waiting. The three men came out too, to watch the pile grow.

Inside, two accumulators were left so I took my red screwdriver and started unscrewing them while Tom and Bill made more trips to the pile in the V in the middle of the two roads, which got bigger and bigger. Then they helped me and the three of us finished the last accumulator and carried it outside together.

The three men moved closer and stood together next to the pile squinting into the sun.

Tom walked over to the pickup and took the axes off the tailgate. He gave one to Bill and one to me.

We stood in front of the pile holding the axes and then Daddy came off the porch. He walked slowly across the grass, looking hard at the three men. They stood together and stretched their necks in their collars and pulled at the neck of their shirts.

"All right," said Daddy. "Go ahead."

The way Tom taught me to swing an ax is that I put my left hand close to the bottom and then slide my right hand up at the same time I swing the ax over my right shoulder. Then, quickly, I pull down with my left hand, sliding my right hand all the way down the smooth wooden handle until it meets my left hand. All the while rolling my right shoulder and swinging my hips to the left, following the pull.

The blades flashed in the sun and sank deep into the Celotex, steel wool, and tin, leaving big gashes in the sides of the accumulators. Tom and Bill were swinging too and then we were all swinging together in the sun *chung chung chung*.

The wooden molding on the sides split easily and after a while some of the panels fell apart under the *chung chung chung* of the axes.

I stopped to rest for a minute. Daddy was still watching the men. He didn't even see us. He was watching them.

We had to chop for a long time so that each panel had a big hole in it or was split. When we were done, Tom walked around the pile, pulling panels with his ax to look for parts we missed. Bill walked over and stood next to Daddy facing the three men. I walked over to Daddy too, and for a while we all watched Tom picking through the pile, except for Daddy who was watching the men.

Daddy said, "That is enough, Mr. Ross."

Tom walked off the pile and stood next to me. The pile was crumpled and broken, and steel wool was hanging out of the panels all frothy and grey.

Daddy's voice was loud, almost a shout, but instead of being loud it was hard and sharp.

"Well, gentlemen. Are you satisfied?"

He waited for a minute. It was perfectly quiet except for some crows on the maple tree next to the barn.

"Would you like us to burn it now?"

The marshal took his hands out of his pockets.

"No, Doctor, I think that will be sufficient."

"Are you sure?" His cheeks were red and his eyes burned.

"Yes, Doctor, I think that is plenty."

"We have gasoline! It would make a nice fire, no?"

"I think we'd better go now, Doctor. We've done what we were supposed to do."

The three men started to walk around the pile to the black car. Daddy left us and walked up to the first man looking at him hard all the time.

"What about books? Not all the books are in New York! There are some here you can burn too! Why not?"

"No, Doctor. Please." The men tried to walk away from him but then they would have walked right into the woods so they kind of walked sideways to their car. One of them took a handkerchief out of his pocket and wiped his forehead. He looked at the sky. The other man licked his lips. The marshal kept trying to look at Daddy but his eyes kept dropping.

"I have more instruments!" Daddy's voice was sharper and made them wince. "Yes, gentlemen. Instruments. Scientific equipment. Would you like to see that on the pile too? No?"

The marshal and one of the men walked around the far side of the black car and got in quickly. The other man, the driver, tried to walk around to the door but Daddy was in front of him. He stood in front of Daddy with his head lowered. Daddy just looked at him. After a long time, the driver raised his head and looked at Daddy and then he dropped his head again.

"Excuse me, Doctor. Please."

"Yes. I'll excuse you. Of course." He stepped aside and the man twisted past him and got into the car.

Daddy walked around and looked at him in the window.

The driver leaned out. His face was white.

"Doctor. I . . . I'm sorry."

"Yes. You're sorry. Of course. Aren't we all. Goodbye, gentlemen. Someday you will understand."

Chapter 3

At times, you have to take some pain and some restriction of happiness; only you should feel, as you do, that happiness is so very important in life. It grows best if you know how to keep yourself clean inside. Then you never lose your ability to be happy, even if things are very sad and lonely at times.

—WR, in a letter, January 25, 1956

Gas was in my eyes in sweet and swirling colors. They were speaking French again but I didn't understand. I didn't understand anything except that the dream was frightening. Waking up I cried because something that happened in the gas was sad. I felt alone and lost in the French hospital.

The young doctor looked at me apologetically and said they had still not been able to get the shoulder back in. This would be the last time, he assured me. He said they were getting more nurses and more attendants and this time they would get it.

Waiting for the others to come and help, I lay back sweating on the table, confused by being afraid of what I had dreamt and at the same time hungry to get back to it. Somehow, by some great mental crossing of the wires deep in the smoky phantasmagoric gas, I had crossed the line between two worlds. The dreams

I could not remember were so close to me and yet I could not understand them. It was something as close and fine as the line of a shimmering horizon separating earth from sky. Sometimes on the tractor with Tom, the closeness between those things hypnotized me. Bumping along on the fender while Tom drove, I used to study the skyline and treetops. During the day it was all one picture of trees and sky. Then as dusk gathered and the sound of the mower fell lower and lower, the leaves and branches lost their detail and became a mass of darkness. All trees were etched against the sky until there was only dark trees and pale sky separated by a bright line. And on the tractor, I was sure there was an upside down, another side, another world from which another little boy could watch a world where the sky was solid and real and the earth was empty. Sometimes I saw him on the other side of the bright line riding the tractor, staring. One day, riding the tractor with Tom in the sunshine I suddenly keeled off the fender and fell into the newly mown grass onto my right shoulder.

And now that same shoulder was in this same dream in this gaseous hospital. Like the sky and the trees, these dreams were pressed together, but I could only see one at a time; enough to know that some other life ran parallel to this one but it was not here. Two stories ran together and mingled their reality. Lying in the cold French hospital, I felt unalive, a reflection. I had seen another life in the gas, and now the nurses were preparing me for death. Three nurses wrapped another sheet around me while the doctor explained: Three nurses would pull on the sheet as if I were in a horizontal hammock, while two doctors pulled on the shoulder to pop it back in the socket. The gas would cushion the muscular agony but oh, my God, what pain and I had cried coming out of the dream because I realized the two realities were not parallel at all, but were aimed to meet at some point in the future.

The mask was snug against my face again over my nose and

mouth and I still had to find out what happened to that other person in the dream. The hissing began and I breathed deeply, sucking hard on the gas. When it began to spin, my forefinger began a slow circle. I had to remember everything. The mask was softer and softer and pressed against my face, making my face softer and softer, losing its shape, melting. But remembering everything. My hand dropped. Everything in the left finger then, holding it up to tell them wait, and then waiting to remember, my mouth and nose growing longer and longer, extending into the mask going after the gas down the pipe like *a deer a deer a deer a deer a deer*

Dull white globes hung over study hall throwing vague shadows out beneath the thirty-five boys all uncomfortable in neckties, sitting in shuffling silence at rows of old-fashioned wooden desks. Some of the boys were studying. Others tried to sleep. Reflected in the black window, Blackman scribbled away at his algebra in front of me. MacGregor was drawing pictures. Hershberger was slouched in his chair trying to read. I was looking at myself. Mr. Hannaford looked up from his desk and then looked away. I looked back at Eutropius.

Mr. Craft, my Latin teacher, had managed to dig up a Latin text for which no pony existed. I didn't like Latin and I didn't feel like doing it. Reaching into my bookbag I pulled out my OROP desert notebook and turned to the last entry: "Oct. 26, 1957: Heavy clouds. Some DOR. Feels like EAs."

I wrote: "Oct. 27. cloudy. Less DOR." I kept a record every day.

I looked at the clock. It was 7:50 and in ten minutes we were all going to the assembly hall for a special meeting. Blackman said he heard that Mr. Hutton was going to announce no school for a few days because of flu. I had already had the flu. Maybe if there was no school for a few days I could go down to

Lewisburg and visit Daddy again. I saw him on October fifth and he said he wanted to give me a secret formula to memorize in case something happened to him. He told me to be brave and I said I would be.

Blackman turned around and quickly dropped a note on my desk. I looked at Mr. Hannaford but he hadn't seen. The note said, "Schwartz says Hutton is just going to give us a sleepover, not close school."

At least a third of the campus, about seventy kids, were in the infirmary or at home. I was in the infirmary for two weeks with Davis. The only time we laughed was when we threw water down the steps to the nurses' office. I told them I couldn't take regular medicine because my father was a special kind of doctor and didn't want me to have regular medicine but they gave me a shot anyway.

I unfolded the last letter I had from Daddy. He said there was a chance he would be paroled November seventh and he would come to school and we would have lunch at Howard Johnson's. I hoped he would come during study hall so I could look out the windows to the road and watch his big Chrysler 300 drive up the long shaded drive. It would feel good to run out and hug him. The last summer we were together in Maine we had gone for a walk and came back to the lower cabin. He told me that the biggest battle was coming and I had to be very strong because he might have to go to jail. Then he stopped by the back door and he said, "Peter, if I go to jail they will think it is a victory for them. But in the end we will win, I am sure of it. But I want you to know that if I have to go to jail I might not come out alive. Do you understand?" I nodded. Then he reached into a little cubbyhole cut into the side of the cabin next to the door and he pulled out his .45. "Peeps," he said, looking at me very seriously, "I want you to know that I am hiding this gun here." He put his hand on my shoulder. "If it gets really bad, I might shoot myself. But it will be all right—I don't know if I will have the courage to face prison." There were tears in his eyes and his hand squeezed my shoulder. "Peeps, sometimes it is so hard." His eyes were very soft and when I hugged him, he cried.

Once he cried in Washington, too. He lived at Alban Towers, a big hotel, and used another name, Walter Roner. It was good to sleep close to him and smell his oil and sometimes we talked in the dark and I watched car lights move around on the ceiling. Actually I liked going to Washington because we went to see things and went to movies a lot. He bought me clothes and model airplanes. He wanted me to go to the Air Force Academy because he said they would look out for me. One night I woke up very late and he wasn't in bed. I heard the typewriter in the study and went out. He was sitting there writing. He looked at me and said, "Peter, they are going to have to come and take me in chains. I won't give up." And then he pulled me close and cried on my shoulder. His hair was soft and white and I patted it for a long time.

The bell rang and everyone jumped up. Blackman waited for me while I folded the letter and then we went to assembly.

Everyone was there. "They even called study hall off for the girls," said Blackman. "I bet it's going to be an important announcement."

"Yeah," I said as we put our books under our seats, "I'm glad I already had the flu, too."

The whole student body, what was left of it, slowly crowded into the assembly hall and rumors passed up and down the rows. Metal chairs squeaked and groaned as students leaned forward whispering what they heard.

Mr. Hutton stood up on the stage and cleared his throat.

"As you all know, we have been hit pretty hard by the flu. The doctors tell us it is going to get worse before it gets better. Therefore, I'm here to tell you that there will be no classes tomorrow."

A cheer went up from the students.

"In fact, there will be no classes for the next two weeks."

The assembly roared as students shouted, clapped, and yelled.

Mr. Hutton waved for silence.

"When you return to your dorms you may call your parents and arrange for transportation. The school will provide a bus to the four o'clock train tomorrow. Those of you who are unable to go home may stay here. One dormitory and the dining hall will remain open. Dismissed."

Hershberger was waiting in line in front of me at the telephone booth in the main dorm.

"Hey Hershberger," I said, "you goin' home?"

He twisted his head sideways and groaned. "Aw, I dunno. My dad has to go to a conference someplace this week and I'm not sure I can afford it anyway." Ed's mother had died a couple of years ago and I told him about Daddy being in jail and we were friends.

"Well look, Ed, if you can't go home, why don't you come home with me? I may be going to see my dad but if that parole comes through, I'll be home most of the time and my mother is a real good cook."

"Well . . ."

"See what your dad says and I'll call my mother right after you."

"Okay."

We pushed and shoved until Ed finally squeezed into the phone booth. He had to talk with his finger in one ear because all the fellows behind me were talking and shouting. We pushed and shoved some more until Ed came out. "Well, I'm not going back to Ohio so I guess I could go home with you."

"Great! Let me call my mother right now."

After I explained about flu vacation I asked Mummy about Ed and she said, "Sure, by all means. I'll come and pick you up tomorrow afternoon after school. I'll probably be there around six."

Upper North was a madhouse as boys raced in and out of rooms, packing and making plans for getting together during vacation. I went into Blackman's room and watched him pack.

"If you come to New York City, you can come over to my place. It's too bad baseball season just ended. I'd like you to see the Yankees play."

"Well, I don't know," I said. "You know Hershberger is coming to my house. And then I may see if I can go and see my dad. . . ."

Blackman paused and then nodded. "Oh yeah. It would be good if you could see him. When is he supposed to get out?"

"Well, maybe November seventh if he gets a parole. The whole sentence was for two years. He's only been in seven or eight months."

"Isn't that an awful long time just for contempt of court?"

I shrugged. "I told you. There were a lot of strange things." Could I tell him about the conspiracy? He wouldn't understand about the HIGs or the EAs or the conspiracy; that Daddy even thought they might be putting him in prison to protect him. How much would Blackman or Hershberger understand?

"Well, didn't he have a good lawyer?"

"No." I laughed proudly. "He didn't trust lawyers. Hell, the prosecutor was a guy who had even been our lawyer for a while. Daddy called him a Judas."

Blackman shook his head. "It sure sounds weird," he said.

"Yeah, I know. There were all kinds of weird things. They sentenced him for two years for contempt and the sentence for contempt is usually only six months. There were all kinds of strange things." And strange things in the prison too. That was why he was going to give me the formula.

The lights blinked, giving us the ten-minute warning.

I stood up just as MacGregor, Blackman's roommate, walked in. "Well, I'm going back to my room. If I can come to New York, I'll give you a call."

"Okay," said Blackman.

"Okay, g'nite."

"Nite."

I lay in my bed for a long time before I went to sleep. My roommate was in the infirmary with flu so I was alone. After a while I got up and went to the window to see if there were any EAs. The night was chilly and there was a cool wind on the lacrosse field behind the dorm. From darkened windows above me and on either side I heard voices as boys finished up last bits of packing by flashlight. Occasionally a proctor's voice cut the mumbling silence.

Bob Blackman and Ed Hershberger were my friends. It was nice having friends but I really wished I could have stayed in Massachusetts where Mummy lived. She said she thought it would be better to go to a boarding school. A lot of the kids came from families that were separated or divorced but it was still lonely because I missed the excitement of going to visit Daddy and being in the country. I wanted Daddy to come and get me. I wanted to be with him in the Corps of Engineers. That was more important than Cheops or Eutropius.

The next day, Hershberger and I walked around campus and watched parents drive up to get their children and watched the school buses leave for the station. The campus was quiet and cold. It already felt like Halloween, spooky and empty. We walked through the empty classrooms and across the empty playing fields, talking. Ed wanted to know more about Daddy.

"If he does get out of prison, what will he do then?"

We had talked of his going incognito and disappearing for a long time, but I wanted him to buy that nice house we always looked at in Maryland. "I don't know what he'll do. He may buy a place near Washington."

"But will his work still be legal? I mean will he still be able to work with that energy?"

"I guess so. I think the thing is that he just can't sell the . . . uh . . . accumulators. Some people call them Orgone boxes. . . ." Even the word Orgone box sounded phony and wrong. Besides, that wasn't why he would be incognito. It was because of the space war. I couldn't tell Ed or Blackman—or even Mummy—how serious the space war was. Daddy said he knew it was serious because the man Ruppelt had written about what happened to him. The Air Force assigned Ruppelt to make a study of the spaceships and the Air Force. One day, while he was working, three men in black suits came and told him to stop working on flying saucers. And then they left. It was a big mystery, said Daddy, the same kind of conspiracy of silence that made the FDA attack us. And it was bigger than accumulators.

"Well, what other kind of stuff is he researching?"

"Unh, he wrote me that in prison he's been doing a lot of mathematics and . . . uh . . . he might even give me some formulas to memorize and keep until he gets out."

It was the formula for negative gravity, and no one would ever know if he really gave it to me or not. That was my insurance. I would never tell anyone if he actually gave it to me because that way if three men in black suits came to get me, they would not kill me, because I had the formula. And one day when Daddy was free I would be a captain or even more in the Cosmic Engineers. When everything was better, they would all drive up in a fleet of cloudbuster trucks, right up the tree-lined driveway, and stop in front of study hall, waiting for me. I would walk out of Latin class or history and get my uniform. All the kids, even the seniors, would be jealous as I went out and saluted my men in the Corps of Cosmic Engineers and we drove off to have cloudbuster bases all over the world. Maybe

they would even come to get me in a flying saucer. Maybe with
the formula we could make friends with them and there wouldn't
be any war any more.

We walked and talked all afternoon. Ed told me about his
family and how he was a conscientious objector. I told him I
was going to the Air Force Academy.

"Well, how come you're going to Oakwood, then? I mean the
Quakers are pacifists, you know."

But the Air Force, well, the Air Force *knew*. They were
going to help me.

"Oh, I'll get in."

It was dark when Mummy came and we loaded the car and
drove on Route 44 back up to Sheffield. I hadn't seen Mummy
since the last time I went to see Daddy and she wanted to know
all about it.

Lewisburg Federal Penitentiary was big and barren. They
let you in through two sets of locked doors so there were always
bars between you and whatever you looked at. Inside the main
hall were high ceilings and shadows on the polished floors.
Around by the entrance were old glass cabinets with wallets
and combs the prisoners made and sold for pocket money. In the
middle of the big hall there was a desk where you signed in
and then you turned left and footsteps followed you down the
hallway.

At the end of the hall was a big room with chairs and couches
in it arranged so that the prisoner sat in a chair in front of the
table and guests sat on the couch opposite. The upholstery was
plain green and red plastic. There was an open space by the
entryway with a black rubber mat. It was a runway for hugging.
Guards stood around by the walls. Daddy wore a blue uniform,
only it was denim and his face was sad. I went with Aurora.
Daddy said they were going to get married in the prison chapel.
He started going to church in prison and sent me prayers and a

piece of the chapel bulletin that had a print of Dürer's praying hands. We talked in low voices. He asked me about school and I said it was okay. He asked me about girls and I told him there had been a girl in Maine, at Bill and Eva's that summer. Her breast fit into my hand just right and made me feel like I was running through the grass. He didn't talk too much about himself, but he said that he heard from one of the other prisoners that he was supposed to have been killed in his cell but for some reason it didn't happen. When the time was up we hugged on the long rubber mat and a guard took him away to a barred door at the end of the room. We watched. After the guard closed the barred door, Daddy turned around in his blue shirt and his eyes reached out all the way across the big room and he gave me his eyes and then he waved and he was gone behind the bars. Footsteps followed us all the way back down the hall.

"It was all right," I said. "Kind of sad."

"Did he ask about me?"

"Yes. He said to send you his love. I wrote you that. That was about all."

"Oh."

I think Mummy was jealous of Aurora. Mummy said she spent fourteen years with Daddy and that was just about the longest any woman had. She tried to go down and visit him once but he didn't want to see her.

Sheffield is a nice little town in the country and we lived in a small apartment on the top floor of a big old New England house right off Route 7. Ed and I had fun together, even did some trick-or-treating on Halloween. We spent the evenings doing homework for Oakwood or watching TV. On Sunday morning, November third, the telephone rang and Mummy answered it. From the bedroom I shared with Ed I heard her say, "Hello? Yes. What?" Then her voice got tight and high. "When? Oh my god. Oh my god."

I ran into the living room and listened. She was crying into the telephone saying "Oh my god, oh my god." I looked at her.

"Mummy. What is it?" She shook her head. "What is it?"

She shook her head. "Oh my god, oh my god."

She had collapsed onto the couch and was holding the telephone, crying.

"Is it Daddy?"

She nodded, rocking back and forth crying into the telephone.

"Is he dead?"

She nodded oh my god.

The morning went by slowly and I watched it all blurred through storm windows. Outside it didn't look as if trees should be moving, but they did, dropping the last leaves on the road and the lawn, clacking branches back and forth with no sound. It was sad to see a window holding so many movements still.

His heart had stopped and they found him in the morning when he didn't show up for roll call. I wanted to know if it had made him wake up or if it just happened. In between telephone calls coordinating how we were to get to Maine for the funeral, it was decided that Mummy would take Ed back to Oakwood and drive up to Maine on the fourth. Bill Steig the cartoonist, and his wife, Kari, driving up from New York, would pick me up in the evening and we would drive all night.

I watched Ed and Mummy through the window as they got in the car and waved, and then I was alone. I went back away from the window and it felt like it did at first when Mummy nodded, that my arms were rising, lifting all by themselves and I would rise with them. My arms were light and empty. They lay on the pillow in front of me and then they smoothed against my eyes, my stomach, and lay my fingers between my legs.

After a while I got up and went to the special brown envelope where I kept notes and mail from Daddy. He had given me a lot of my own papers to keep. I put them out on the table and looked at them.

The first thing was a poem. It was in my own handwriting:

> On a mound
> On the ground
> On a hill lies
> The body of a great man
> Thoughts—
> To one side he cried
> And thought of the life he led
> As it grew late he thought of Orgonon
> The great which
> he discovered then
> He thinks of his
> Son whom he loved
> So, on the hill
> On the ground
> In a mound, he rests
> Thinking.

And with it, the exact same poem copied in Daddy's handwriting. At the end it said, "Peter wrote this Feb. 27, 1954."

There was a picture I took of tubes from a DORbuster in the bathtub in Washington showing the energy field around the pipes.

Then there was another poem. On top of the page was "CCA—Cloudbuster CORE of America." The poem read:

A Poem by Peter Reich

> The dry lands will soon be wet
> with a special gentle rain
> for people who have important crops.

> On the cloudseeders we will gain
> for their silly old "rain"
> and those funny cloud makers.

> On top of all this
> Mushy mush
> Just one man will do it all alone.

And then in my handwriting: Dear Daddy here is a poem for you Pete.

A couple of telegrams from the trial telling me to be brave, and telling me to keep my belly soft. The picture of Dürer's hands. Daddy wrote on it:

To Pete to pray from
May 10, 1957, Dad.

Outside it was raining and it was almost dark. Cars went past on Route 7 and their headlights wobbled on the ceiling. The trees reached up into the sky barely moving. But there was no sound.

The Steigs arrived after it was dark. The big green finned Plymouth drove in the driveway and I met them at the door under a light that dripped with rain. Kari was pregnant. We drove up through the night with the dashboard glowing green on our faces. We talked quietly about things that had happened and what would happen. Kari said she felt good going to the funeral carrying a child.

The day of the funeral was grey and I wore a black suit and a red tie and the floor was red. Tom had waxed the linoleum floor so it was shiny and held onto people's legs. Bill and Dr. Baker arranged the funeral and it all happened in dark shadows on the linoleum. Outside there were yellow and red leaves on the ground and I went underneath a dripping spruce tree to kick at the dirt and look for something I remembered burying once. The leaves held shiny still drops on their bellies. We got a record player so we could play "Ave Maria" and other music and the label on the record was red but not as red as the floor. In the middle of the floor the casket was a soft copper color. Outside it was blowing and drizzling. I watched the clouds for a minute but the floor was so red. Dr. Baker got up to say something with his feet sinking into the linoleum. My shoes turned around and ran up the carpet upstairs to where the carpet was soft purple and rough on my hands and cheeks, my burning cheeks. I lay on the floor of the study for a long time whispering come back come back and when I got up there was a red spot in the carpet.

Outside the wind was cool on my cheeks and hair and there were many faces moving around all hunched up in shoulders against the November wind. The wind was blowing and someone was standing on top of the tomb getting ready to lower the casket down. Leaning against the wall to put on top of the tomb was a big piece of plywood. It was yellow and the wind was going to blow it over. I held it up as the casket went down. I wanted to put Daddy's razor in it so he could shave. Then some men came and took the plywood, grunting as they lifted it on top of the tomb. Then they put a carpet over the plywood and put Daddy's bust on the carpet. The carpet was red.

Afterward I helped Bill clean up. We went upstairs to the study and I looked out of the window. Clouds stumbled over each other to run across the sky fastest and sometimes rain came and fell against the window streaking the windows and my face. Bill came over to me and put his arm around me. We both looked out of the window for a while watching the last leaves blow off the trees. He squeezed my shoulder.

"Well, Peter," he said slowly, "I guess you're a captain now."

His voice was soft in the quiet of the study, and it made me feel better. The soft wooded walls were so quiet without the big clock ticking. The war was over and even though Daddy had said we won I didn't feel as though we won. Outside the trees were empty and the soldiers were gone.

"Yeah," I said, trying to smile bravely, "and I guess you're a colonel."

On the way back down to New York, we stopped at Bill and Eva's. The sky had cleared on the way down from Rangeley and after dinner I took the old beat-up Stetson and went outside alone. It was dark and bright with a cool wind. A sliver of moon hung abandoned in the empty branches. In the garden, dry golden cornstalks wobbled shoulders together.

Toreano waited for me on his pony, half hidden in the shadow of the barn. He waited until I came away from the house and then nudged his pony into the brighter darkness.

I tugged at the brim of the Stetson, pulling it down over my eyes.

"It's been a long time," I said slowly.

He nodded and waited for me to say more. The fringes on his deerskin jacket swayed as the pony leaned down to nibble on wet grass.

"Are they ready?"

He nodded again. It had been so long since I had been with Toreano and the men. I felt older and sadder. My battle scars were inside me. There was a kind of battle fatigue, a feeling like after pressing my arms against a doorjamb, when they rise all by themselves with a tired lightness. I really hadn't spent time with Toreano since the summer after the trial when I visited Daddy at Orgonon. We played some cowboy-and-Indian games but it bored us sometimes. Once in a while he guarded while I walked naked in the grass. On some sunny hot days he brought the Indian Princess out of the forest and she was earth grass and wind beneath soft tall trees or in a place where deer had slept, a gentle brown hollow in the grass where the earth felt good to my legs. The princess was soft and graceful and I held on tighter and tighter until I was sweating and relaxed. The wind made all the fuzzy grass brush against my skin and cool it and the soft wet moss was sparkling in the sun.

We ran together in the back fields, climbing trees to look around for Indians, charging across the hospital field and galloping down the dusty road toward home.

In the evenings Daddy and I walked together in the fields

with our rifles and then the scouts and cavalry waited in the shadows of the forest in case something happened. We had good talks, walking quietly across the fields with our rifles, sometimes shooting a squirrel or a porcupine. I walked there after the funeral. It seemed a long time ago, and tucked in between a small cluster of fields looking west toward the hospital field, there was a wooden chair. It had warped and the finish was almost weathered away. He must have come there to sit when he was alone. All alone at Orgonon. With Toreano watching.

I wanted to ask Toreano what it was like then, when I was not there and he was there alone, riding at easy gallop behind Daddy's big white car. I wanted to know if he had seen Daddy cry when he sat in that chair, and if he still played the organ letting the music float out and mingle with the air. I wanted him to tell me what it was like to stand, as I ordered him to stand, at the top of the stairway in the observatory, watching Daddy work and look out of the windows.

Toreano shifted in his saddle as if he were uncomfortable with my silence as I watched the sky. Yes, this was the cavalry.

"Well," I said, straightening up, "let's get on with it."

I started walking to the cloudbuster platform that Bill and Eva had built next to their garden. Toreano rode ahead of me. His pony was skittish and whinnied as he reined to a halt next to the platform. I could feel his eyes watching me as I slowly climbed the stairs onto the platform.

Standing at the edge, facing west, I could see way across the dry tops of the cornstalks into the western sky. The men stood very still, at rest, with their eyes on me. Most of them were very young. They hadn't been there for many of the battles. Their eyes shone with a kind of respect I wasn't used to. They would be good soldiers. And brave. My fingers traced the soft wood of the railing as I tried to think of words.

"Men. Some of you were in battle and some of you are new. Many of you will be able to tell your children about what has happened. And you should be proud. You men are part of the newest outfit in the world, the Cosmic Engineers, and you have experienced things that most people wouldn't understand. Together, we have opened up a whole new world for exploration. First with the cloudbuster, making rain, and then, when the flying saucers began to attack, with the spacegun.

"And most of you know what happened then. They put the general in jail and he died. They were afraid of the truth and they killed him. So now the big battle is over. We've come over a new horizon into a new way of thinking and feeling. But it will be a long time, men, before we are ready to fight again."

My voice choked and I felt a terrible emptiness inside, like losing something. Only it wasn't like losing something because when you lost something it just got lost and you didn't know until it was already lost. And now I felt sad because I knew I was going to lose something and in some funny way I knew I had to lose it myself and that made it harder because if I lost it on purpose, it meant that I would always know where to find it again, even if I couldn't. It was something I didn't understand, but had to.

"And so the reason Toreano called you here tonight is because we're going to break up the outfit. You can keep your rifles and your uniforms. Use your horses to start farms. Raise families. Be good citizens. But always be ready. Raise your children free and happy and let them be ready for the next time because they will be the children of the future." The wind rose sharply and the men nodded their heads, turning to look at the wind. "I . . ." was very sad ". . . am going to miss you all. But we will be together again. I know it. We are on the side of truth. Thank you."

I stood up straight, at attention, and looked at them for a long time. They all looked at me. I waited for a minute until the wind died down, and then very slowly and very seriously I saluted.

"Dismissed."

The formation broke up quietly and Toreano and I watched them go to their horses, mount and ride away in all the directions there are. We could hear their saddles creaking for a long time. When they were gone, Toreano nudged his pony up so that he was sitting directly in front of me. His eyes were full of words.

I wanted to ask him what he really thought. If he thought we had really won, and where he would go, what he would do. But I knew we would meet again.

"Goodbye, Toreano. I . . ."

He smiled quietly and his eyes flashed underneath the dark brim of his hat. We looked at each other for a long time. Then he leaned forward in the saddle holding his hand out to mine. We shook hands firmly. He flicked the reins and was gone.

I watched the wind carry him into the night and for a long time I stood on the platform watching the stars turn over and over in the sky. I shivered. I felt alone, and I knew I would be alone for a long long time.

Every night after lights out I went to the window to watch for EAs because they were going to come and take me away. One would land on the lacrosse field behind the dormitory and I would know and they would know and Daddy would be inside, happy again, smiling.

Sometimes, if I felt really bad, I snuck up to Blackman's room. Blackman would lie in bed and I'd sit by the window and we'd talk. He was my best friend. Once, when I cried, he held my hand all night. We talked a lot.

"Oh. Watching the sky again?"

"Yeah." Clouds separated the stars.

"Well, what happens if you see one?"

"I mark it down in my notebook. You see, we sort of have to keep a record of everything."

"Is it all supposed to mean something?"

It means they are going to come and get me, it means everything is all right. That is how they came and got Jesus because they knew he knew and they got Daddy and Daddy won't leave me alone here because he loves me.

"Well, it means that spacemen are sort of keeping an eye on earth."

"What for? Are they going to take it over?"

Maybe. But now that they have Daddy, they know what was happening and the DOR will stop. The attacks will stop. The war will be over. We can be friends.

"No, it isn't to take it over so much, I guess, just to observe mostly, and see what was happening on earth. They're friendly." Clouds flew away and the sky over the lacrosse field was clear, stars sparkling in the cold November night. Blackman was quiet for a long time. Then he said, "Hey Reich. Do you really believe there is something out there?"

I nodded solemnly. "I really do."

"Do you believe in God?"

"No, I guess I don't believe in a regular God."

"Well, what do you believe in then?"

I sighed and looked out into the stars. They twinkled and glowed. "I believe in a kind of cosmic mind, I guess."

"You mean like in philosophy books where a guy has a kind of abstract idea of something bigger but not as definite as God?"

"No, I mean that there is actually a thing out there." The stars seemed brighter now, as if they were answering me. "A real mass of plasma floating around in space. It's probably huge, as big as the solar system or the galaxy, but big, and it is all mind. It is all thinking and feeling."

"Is that like heaven?"

I thought about that for a while. It was a nice idea because it would be a place where there was nothing but thinking and feeling inside the big pulsating plasma. It would feel good forever.

"Yeah, I guess it would be like heaven."

And Daddy would be there, his mind free. He was so sad at the end, when we walked and talked together. He was like a man who was standing on top of the world looking over into a new world. That is what Daddy was like. He had lifted himself so he was looking over the horizon to a new world, a free and happy world. He stood there on the edge of the universe looking into the future, and when he turned around to say, "Come on, let's go," they pulled the ladder out from under him and killed him.

I turned around and looked at Blackman's bunk. All I could see was a round lump of blankets.

"Blackman, do you believe in God? . . . Blackman?"

He was asleep.

The days passed sadly. Sometimes at my typewriter, I got garbled messages from Daddy about MODJU and HIGs and Christ and I knew he would come soon. It happened the night that Blackman and MacGregor fixed up a special thing on the doorknob of their room.

They spent all afternoon after classes wiring the radio so that the wires came around the door frame and, when the door was closed, completed the connection in the door latch. When the door was closed the radio was on and when the door was open it was off.

Blackman dusted his hands off. "Well, that will drive him crazy. He'll never be able to figure it out."

We tried it a few times and it worked like a dream. As soon as you turned the doorknob, the radio went off. MacGregor stood around tapping his thumb against his fingertips nervously.

"Hey," he said. "Do you think we ought to have a rope ladder ready so we can escape when he gets mad? Ha ha. Hey Reich, why don't you get your flying saucers to come and rescue us when Herm figures it out. Ha ha."

Herm was a big Persian who was the proctor on Upper North.

He was a senior who had weights under his bed. He was very strong and sometimes didn't understand what was happening. That night I went to the john after lights out on a reconnaissance mission to find out what kind of mood Herm was in. He was standing, as usual, in front of the mirrors in his underpants, flexing his muscles.

"How ya doin', Herm?" I said, peeing into the urinal.

"Ah," he said, grinning at himself in the mirror. "Good."

He had a big hairy chest and hairy arms and hairy everything. He even had hair on his shoulders and it moved as he wiggled his shoulder muscles. He grinned again. "Ah. Good."

I walked over to the sink to wash my hands and Herm turned to me. He lifted his right leg and held his calf out to me.

"Hey," he said, "feel dat."

"What?"

"Here. Feel dat." He put my hand on his calf and tightened the muscle. "Dat's a focking brick. Just like a focking brick. Eh?"

"Yeah, Herm, you sure are strong. Well, g'nite."

I tiptoed up the stairs and hurried into Blackman and MacGregor's room.

"Is he okay?" asked Blackman.

Sliding under Blackman's bunk, I said, "Yeah, he's real happy looking at his muscles."

"Okay, then he shouldn't get too mad, right?"

"Right."

"Ha ha." MacGregor giggled in his upper bunk.

"Okay, here goes the radio." Blackman flicked the radio on, and soft low rock and roll poured out of the room through the closed door into the hall.

Blackman and MacGregor pulled their covers up pretending to be asleep. I pulled my legs in underneath the bunk. The room was dark and we waited for Herm.

After a few minutes, we saw the shadows of his feet standing in front of the door as he listened. The door flew open.

"*Hey!*" Herm shouted. "No radio after lights out. Unnerstan'?"

MacGregor leaned wearily out of his bunk. "Huh? Hey Herm, what are you talking about? Radio? We're trying to sleep. C'mon."

"Yeah," murmured Blackman. "C'mon."

Under the bed, I gasped.

"Well, I tot I heard radio. Sorry."

He closed the door and we all exploded in laughter. Then we held our breath and listened to Herm's feet pad down the hall.

"Turn it up," said MacGregor. "Ha ha."

Blackman held the radio under his covers and turned it up good and loud.

From under the bed I saw the shadows of Herm's feet come back and stand in front of the door.

I started giggling. Then I was laughing so hard I couldn't breathe. The bed rocked as Blackman and MacGregor laughed too.

Herm's fist closed on the door and he burst into the room. Silence. Well, almost silence. I could hear Blackman and MacGregor eating their pillows.

Herm looked around the room with a low growl.

"Aaaaarghh."

Then he closed the door. Bam. The rock and roll screamed into the room.

> Come along an' be my party doll
> Come along an' be my party doll.

The door flew open and Herm stood, feet parted in the doorway, snarling.

"Aaaaarrghh. Wot is dis?" he muttered. The bed rocked with laughter, but the room was quiet.

Herm closed the door slowly. It was perfectly quiet until the latch hit the metal frame.

> Come along an' be my party doll
> I wan' make love to you to you

Herm burst in and looked into the silent room. Then he closed the door again

I wan' make love to you

It opened again fast and then he stood there in the hallway slamming and opening the door, chopping up sound

I want

SLAM!

to make love

SLAM!

to you!

WHAM! The door burst open.

"Turn it off!" screamed MacGregor. Blackman, clutching the radio beneath his blankets, turned it off. I was a tiny ball under the bed.

Herm roared. "Wot da fock? Where's da radio? Wot da fock goin' on?"

Blackman tried to look sleepy but his laugh broke through.

"Uh. Hi Herm. Ha ha we ha we haha were just trying to uh ha ha fix the radio . . ."

"Fix da radio. Fock da radio. Where's MacGregor?" He walked over to MacGregor's bunk and ripped him out of bed. Holding him with one fist in the middle of the room he started to shake him.

"What da fock you doin'? Ha?"

MacGregor wobbled as Herm shook him, but he couldn't stop laughing, which just made Herm madder.

"We weren't doing anything, Herm, honest. Blackman was just trying to fix the radio. Honest. Ha ha."

Underneath the bed, I was crying with laughter, my legs doubled up against my chest.

"Focking pricks. Focking pricks. Make fun of Herm. I show you. Arrggghhh." He drove MacGregor against the wall and Blackman hopped out of bed.

"Hold it, Herm. Wait, don't kill him! Wait!"

He started pulling at Herm, but Herm started pushing him toward the window. Blackman turned to catch himself and then he shouted, "Holy shit! Look at that!"

Herm stopped shaking MacGregor and looked out the window. Under the bed I stopped laughing.

"Hey Reich," said Blackman. "Look at this. Man are they here tonight."

I slid out from under the bed and squeezed in between them to look out of the window. Three red and green balls were flying in tight formation in the sky over the lacrosse field, flashing, glowing, and signaling.

Herm let MacGregor slide to the floor. "Wot da fock? Wot's going on?" He looked around the room with a puzzled expression and then back out the window. "Foist da radio and den da lights. Wot . . . ? Hey Reich," he shouted, pointing a hairy fist at me. "Wot da fock you doin' here? Get da fock out!"

Gladly.

I raced downstairs as fast as I could and whipped into my room. Putting on a jacket, pants, and shoes, I opened the window and jumped out onto the lacrosse field.

The EAs were low in the sky and didn't seem very far away. They were green and red balls, flitting around in the sky coming closer and closer. Coming to take me away at last.

The November wind cooled the tears of laughter on my face and now my eyes began to burn. I walked out across the field toward the EAs. Behind me I heard the murmur of voices as boys leaned out of their windows to watch the balls in the sky. From his window in Upper North, I heard Blackman call, "Hey Reich! Where are you going! Come back! Come back!"

But I ignored him. The flying saucers were coming to take me away. I had to let them know I was here. If I concentrated hard enough and thought real hard, they would catch my signal. I saw them bobbing in the sky, quivering. My eyes were in give give and they went up through the sky and the wind saying please come and take me away to the stars, please come please come.

Inside the spaceship it was all silver-blue light and there were men standing at the controls. The walls were glowing silver blue except where there were Orgone Radar Screens. The spaceship was filled with the soft hum of the Orgone Motor. The men were in silver blue too, with serious faces as they looked down through the scope at Earth, at Oakwood, and at the lacrosse field.

It could land right over there at the end of the field if I could only signal them. There must be a signal in case they don't know. What if Daddy is in the spaceship? How will they know if it is really me and not a spy? I remembered the photograph of the two hands making an energy field, hanging in the observatory. As I walked to the end of the field I started making the energy field with my hands, holding them out in front of me, palms facing. Slowly I brought them together and then apart until I felt the energy field between them. They would be able to see it on the scope.

Inside the spaceship, the men were preparing to bring it down on the field. The silver-blue light made a soft grey shadow as the captain's hands moved across the control panel. The energy from his fingertips made small lights blink on and off. The spaceship started a wobbly descent. Daddy looked through the scope and he could see me. He wasn't wearing his khaki pants and red-and-black checkered shirt. They were in mothballs at Bill and Eva's house in Maine. He was wearing a new uniform made of silky blue, with the spinning wave symbol across his chest. On his shoulders were general's stars, only these were real stars, five on each side, glowing and sparkling. His face was pink and looked calm and serene as he looked through the scope.

In the night I walked across the field, making the energy field with my hands, praying that he would come and take me away, Please come, I said, looking long and hard at the glowing balls coming nearer out of the sky. Please come and take me away please please. Please, here are my eyes, here I am sending them far out to you. To You. Giving my eyes, please come please. Far away in the sky there was a noise. I heard a dog bark.

Daddy's eyes were soft and smiling. He was happy because he was going to come and take me away with him to another planet where we would be happy and free. This world wasn't ready for him. In a new language without words, in a language of thought, the navigator looked at Daddy. Daddy went over to the Orgone Radar Screen that glowed with red and blue specks of light. He could see the three blips from the spaceships and below them, a faint blip where I was making the energy field as a beacon. Then at the corner of the screen he saw what the navigator had seen: the cold hard blips of Air Force jets.

The jets came from the south. They were closing in fast with blinking lights and a dull roar. My hands stopped going in and out and I stared in horror. The jets were going to chase them away! O my God, didn't they understand that these flying saucers weren't enemies now? That they had Him? O God, please don't let them chase him away. Please come quickly. Come quickly to the field and take me. Oh, please, please. I started running across the field while at the other side of the sky the jets circled to take bearings and then they started to close on the spaceships. I watched the sky from the middle of the earth.

Daddy's face was still as he watched the radar screen and saw the jets come closer and closer. Then he moved back to the other scope and watched me standing in the field, running and stopping,

looking up and moving my hands in and out. Give me your eyes,
Peeps, he whispered. The captain thought to Daddy and told him
they had to move fast or the jets would strike. Daddy thought at
me in the screen. Peter, we cannot come and save you. You must
be brave and stay here on Earth. His tears, when they hit the
soft blue screen, made little soft noises. I'm sorry, Peeps, sonny.
We have to go. They still don't believe it, but we won. We won.
Goodbye, Peeps, goodbye. I will always love you. He looked at
the captain and nodded.

The balls disappeared very fast, moving into the northeast
corner of the sky. They vanished while the jets flew in swirls and
webs across the sky.

The nurses unwrapped me. Slowly they loosened the sheet. I
was crying. My body was intact. My shoulder was back again
but I am crying too, thinking *a deer a deer a deer*

Part two

Chapter 4

Le pur enthousiasme est craint des faibles âmes
Oui ne sauraient porter son ardeur ni son poids.
Pourquoi le fuir?—La vie est double dans les flammes.
D'autres flambeaux divins nous brûlent quelquefois:
C'est le Soleil du ciel, c'est l'Amour, c'est la Vie;
Mais qui de les éteindre a jamais eu l'envie?
Tout en les maudissant, on les chérit tous trois.

ALFRED DE VIGNY (1797–1863)
"La Maison du Berger"

Looking out over the Maine countryside from the top of the hill, at the end of a gently curving path and gathered in among trees, stood the tomb. It was big, about ten feet long and five feet wide. Its walls of cemented rock resembled those of the larger rock building at the other end of the path, only instead of a gravel porch on top, the tomb was covered with a slab of salt-and-pepper granite. Cut thick, the granite top looked like a real roof: a peak extended down the middle creating a slight pitch and giving the rain a place to fall from, out away from the rock walls.

In the middle of the granite, on the side of the roof that sloped out toward open countryside, was bolted a larger-than-life bust.

Sitting next to the bust on top of the hard speckled granite, one might have let one's eye be drawn over two or three miles of spruce, fir, and birch forest to where Hunter Cove brought Rangeley Lake into view at the base of sloping pastures. On a clear day, Mount Washington and New Hampshire's White Mountains gleamed on the southwest horizon. It was a good view, carefully maintained and held above groping young tree tops by Tom Ross's ax.

Nearly ten years after the death of the man who first hired him to care for that land, Tom Ross was the only one who remained. Salaried by a trust fund created by the will, he served that part of the will which established a museum and provided for upkeep of the grounds. In summer, from 9 A.M. to noon and 2 P.M. to 4 P.M. on Tuesdays and Thursdays, Tom Ross and his wife, Bea, showed visitors through the museum. The rest of the time he mowed lawns, maintained the buildings, looked after his grandchildren and great-grandchildren (a growing brood), and worried about social security. On snowshoes in winter, he went back into the forests of Orgonon with his ax to trim trees. Working slowly and carefully with measured strokes of his ax, he cleared away underbrush and dead branches so the forests would grow straight and tall around the shoulders of the hill.

Striking out at random from the tomb, a walker might suddenly have stumbled out of thick undergrowth into the silent parts that Tom had trimmed. Or the walker might have found other signs of activity: small holes and piles of rocks scattered about; one of many old garbage dumps hidden and forgotten beneath trees, crawling with roots, needles and moss; old cedar fences covered with thick green moss; strange circles.

The circles were barely distinguishable among blueberry bushes, squaw bush, and baby evergreens, their ragged circumference held by the soft blurry limits of a strange moss that grew wherever there had been a fire in the ground.

Clouds of smoke boiled out of the trees like soft white balloons until there was nothing left to see except snow.

Everything was white. On the other side of the brush fire, leaves crackled and branches broke as Tom threw armfuls of brush onto the hissing fire.

The white smoke came up around me from the fire softer than snow crunching underneath my boots. I threw a branch into the smoke and squinted away. The smoke made it harder to breathe. Daddy made it easier.

"Pete!" Tom hollered to me. He couldn't see me for the smoke. "What!"

"You okay?" His boots crunched in the snow and got closer. Then his hat and face came out. "Here! Lie down on the snow."

He put his ax down and kneeled down. It looked like he was floating in the smoke. "Lie down," he said again, lying down on the snow.

I put my ax down too and lay down. Suddenly the air was clear and I could breathe and see. Where we lay down there was about a foot of clear air like a blanket between the snow and the smoke. Tom held onto his ax with one hand and took a bite of tobacco with the other. He grinned and held the tobacco out to me. I shook my head. Tom shook his head too and grinned. He always offered it to me. Past Tom, tree trunks broke out of the snow and disappeared into the smoke. The fire crackled and hissed but we couldn't see it.

"Hey Tom. How come the smoke doesn't reach all the way to the ground?"

"Oh, I dunno. That's how lumberjacks keep out of the smoke, 'cause it is always clear air right over the top of the snow."

The crust was rough to my cheek and if I moved my leg or my arm the crust crunched. Animal footprints and broken pieces of leaves were frozen into the crust around us and a cold smell came up through. I pulled the ax closer to me and smelled the handle. It smelled like pitch and smoke rubbed in by Tom's big hands.

"Hey Tom. Are we going to cut any more trees today?"

"Oh, I dunno. I guess we'll let this burn down and go into town for the afternoon mail. You aren't cold, are you?"

I shook my head. He grinned and raised his head to spit and check the fire. I wondered how far the smoke went into the forest and what it looked like from up above where there wasn't any smoke. Maybe just the tops of the trees were sticking out of the top of the smoke like a forest of tiny Christmas trees. It was almost Christmas but I didn't want it to come until the third thing happened. Mummy always said bad things happened in threes and we already had two.

In 1966, Tom Ross was still at Orgonon, retracing paths through the woods that only he knew, mowing lawns in summer, burning brush in winter, keeping Orgonon clean and neat, stopping over on weekends and after hours to make sure no one broke in.

The new fad, snowmobiles, made the buildings more accessible in winter, and although there had been no major thefts one or two break-ins had occurred. Once, someone slashed some paintings. No one in the region knew how much to believe about what was in the buildings, although rumor had it that there was a lot of scientific equipment and some pretty nice furniture. Beyond the rumors and what was immediately visible to museum visitors, it was hard to know what was still there. No doubt something of a Frankenstein quality lingered in the minds of these villagers —eager to promote tourism in their region—who for nearly fifteen years had listened to the thick foreign accents of the doctors and scientists out there doing experiments with . . . ENERGY.

Tom Ross had been through it all and now he remained there, a link between past and present. Working alone there all those years he must have gone over the events and people carefully, because as time passed and more people came to see Orgonon, his stories expanded and lengthened. He spoke quietly and lovingly of The Doctor, telling stories that showed fairness, honesty, imagination, and error. Wisely, Tom refused to speak into the new-fangled tape recorders that some people brought.

Ironically, in 1966, Tom Ross was one of the few people who could talk about The Doctor. Many of the others, both with accents and without, who had participated in The Doctor's American years were silent, ruminating over the years with Reich. Some were bitter at the world, some were uncertain about the future, others strived in their own way to continue research into a body of work they considered immensely valuable.

Physicians in countries all over the world were making careful slow discovery of Reich's work, always pushing back and re-arranging dates and periods to redefine what was "acceptable." In 1966, psychiatrists in training were still being told to stop reading *Character Analysis* halfway through "because that was when Reich went mad."

If sanity was a trivial issue separating the world of traditional medicine and science from Reich's work, the followers of Reich had their own quarrels which, in the perspective of history, would also seem trivial. Unwilling to accept labels such as "disciple" or "Reichian," a number demanded orthodoxy and defied defini-tion with such vigor that their assertions sometimes made them appear as worshipers or fanatics.

On an international level, there was no communication at all between interested students. In America, divisive power plays, lawsuits, and quarrels typified relations among many who felt themselves to be the heirs of Reich's legacy.

And a good many were silent.

One of those who was quiet was Eva Reich. After her father's death, she and her husband, William Moise, went to live in a small community on the coast of Maine. For many years Eva was busy with an organic garden, reading, and her daughter. Bill became a full-time artist. He delved into color with his fingers and created paintings that radiated with patterns of moving light.

As issues and arguments rose and fell around Reich's work, Eva developed what she called "an unearthly detachment" from the infighting. She worked hard to make birth control and sex education more accessible to young people and poor people throughout the state of Maine, but she refused to be drawn into the quarrels about her father's legacy. "These are the power politics after the emperor dies," she said once after discussing a legal question. "The basic scientific principles are more important than the power politics." The core of the work, she said, would endure longer than the personal struggles.

Tom Ross was another who steered clear of the personal struggles. Extending the line of cleared forests and manicured lawns each year, he knew better than anyone that his work would endure; it would be a forest someday. Fully competent in his field and well above the power struggles, Tom might have had interesting observations on those others who occasionally reappeared out of the past to walk around Orgonon, go out to look at the tomb, reminisce with him. Few, if any, ventured into the woods, where there were many treasures, but most of them enjoyed talking with Tom as much as he enjoyed the interruptions from his routine and the opportunity to talk about The Doctor.

In October of 1966, he saw a group of young people coming across the property. Among them he recognized Peter, the son. Tom was glad to see him.

Orgonon was lonely without all the people. When we got back from town I went up to the hill to see if the smoke was still there in the snow but it was gone. All I could see from the observatory steps were fields and trees all white and still and quiet. It smelled like snow, lonely. The rooms were always cold. Everyone left after Oranur. Oranur was the first bad thing. There had to be three before Christmas.

Oranur was when Daddy put a radium needle in the big accumulator in the lab and everyone got sick. The lab closed, the mice died. People went away. The air was so bad I had to take a bath every day and have blood tests. A lot of people got sick. Eva got sick. Mummy had to go away for a long time. She was sick too. I missed her a lot. Then she came back. I wanted her to stay.

The instruments were still and quiet in the big room downstairs in the observatory. After the lab was closed all the instruments were moved up the hill. The red linoleum floor was soft, cold grey.

I tiptoed upstairs. Daddy was sitting at his desk working. I waited at the top of the stairs underneath the picture of two hands making an energy field.

After a while, he looked at me over the top of his glasses.

"Hi, Peeps." He smiled.

"Hi, Daddy."

"I'm glad you came. We can have a talk after I finish this. Why don't you read a book."

I got out the Sears and Roebuck catalogue and sat down next to the fireplace. They had a really nice two-gun set and all kinds of cowboy boots. I liked the ones with pointed toes.

After a while the pen stopped scratching and Daddy came over to the fireplace. I built a fire like Tom showed me and we sat together in front of the fire looking at the catalogue.

"What do you want for Christmas?" asked Daddy.

"I want a two-gun set!"

"But I just gave you that nice holster set last year. Why do you want another? What more do you want?"

I wanted a two-gun set. I turned the pages to the cowboy boots. The cowboy boots had red and yellow swirls in the sides. Roy Rogers tucked his pants in but real cowboys didn't. Mummy said she would get me cowboy boots for Christmas.

"How about a little golden watch?"

"A what?"

"A little golden watch for the little prince?"

"I'm not a prince." I turned the page hard. Sometimes he teased me about being a prince and it made me confused. All I really wanted was a two-gun set and cowboy boots. And a cowboy hat.

"It will be harder when you grow up," said Daddy.

We turned to the pictures of ladies standing up and smiling in soft white underwear. I liked the soft curves of their breasts and the warm soft way the white part was close to their skin. All the ladies were smiling at us. Daddy said, "Do you have a girl friend?"

It always made me funny when he asked that because I didn't know what he meant. The ladies in the picture smiled at us and held their hands in funny positions. They stood in long rows of clothing.

"Well, not really I guess. I like Candy a lot. And Kathleen." Kathleen and I played Roy Rogers and Dale Evans.

"Have you kissed them?"

Some of the ladies in the Sears and Roebuck held their hands up in the air like they were pointing to the ceiling.

"No. . . ."

He looked down at the rows of ladies and pointed to a nice one. "Do you like her?"

She was pretty. Her hands pointed off to the side as if she was going to turn around and then walk right out of the Sears and Roebuck catalogue so she could come and sit next to us on the couch wearing a soft white slip.

"Yes, she is pretty," I said. I looked at the fire and thought that if it were magic, when I looked back at the couch she would be sitting there in a white slip, smiling at Daddy with her fingers pointed at the ceiling.

Daddy said, "Are you glad that Mummy came back?"

She disappeared. Over the fireplace was the picture Daddy

painted of an eagle standing alone high on a mountain looking over the world. I nodded.

She had to go away. She said it was because she got sick after Oranur and had to have an operation. Sometimes when Daddy got mad he yelled at her and said he hated her and wanted her to go away. Everybody went away after Oranur. I wanted her to come back but I didn't want them to fight. I had to stay with Daddy for the three bad things.

As they walked across the rolling Maine fields that autumn weekend in 1966, the young people who accompanied Peter felt strange. As a group they knew little about Dr. Reich and had no idea what had ended at Orgonon nine years earlier. They saw only abandoned, decaying buildings and a quiet caretaker. There was something dreamlike about the place: some strange things had happened here with a strange and unearthly kind of energy.

One or two of the guests, who had notions of Reich as some old Victorian type, were surprised to find Orgonon decidedly rough-hewn. In the cabin they used, the cabin Peter had inherited, the knotty-pine walls and open fireplace led one of the group to describe Orgonon as having a distinctly American quality.

But the mood of the place was more complicated than simple, honest American dilapidation. Behind the locked doors of those buildings lurked the disquieting mystery of that energy.

Exploring the grounds together, they learned—although not from Peter—that the long, low building called the laboratory was closed and had been unused since 1952, when an unusual experiment called Oranur was conducted. The building could not be used because it still carried a charge from that experiment with energy.

At different locations around the property, on large wooden

platforms, stood great gunlike machines with rows of long dull aluminum pipes extending like barrels. The guests were told this apparatus was used in experiments to control atmospheric energy.

Wandering around the cabin, one of the group, a young psychologist from Boston named Ed Carmel, found the place haunted with energy things. In a corner he found a casting of the same bust they had seen on top of the tomb. This bust, it was explained to him, was given to Peter by a physician who found that its presence put a high energy charge in his home. He could not keep it in his own house because it seemed to "radiate energy."

The six visitors were perplexed by the ominous presence of this energy everywhere, and the more they sought answers to their questions, the more they were frustrated. Most unnerving to them was their host, Peter, at twenty-two silent and uncomfortable about what had happened here. Much of what they learned about what transpired years ago came from a young law student named Peter d'Errico, who had roomed with Peter in college. Several times during the weekend, the others had the very distinct feeling that d'Errico was acting as a kind of interpreter for his former roommate. D'Errico had spent a summer working in Rangeley and during that time learned much about Dr. Reich. He told them what he could about Reich's work in atmospheric research, the Food and Drug Administration injunction, Reich's refusal to comply, the trial, imprisonment. He explained that because of the legal complications, much of Reich's later work remained untested and unexplored. But even he was confused by Peter's behavior, his silence and uneasiness.

One afternoon, the seven were walking up past the lab and turned off the road to walk through the autumn-browned fields. The road split. They left the crumbling asphalt road that led up to the observatory and took a faded tractor trail out between trees to the back fields. Suddenly, Peter walked away from them. He stood in the middle of the V created by the two diverging roads and looked at them. Then he looked at the ground. There was nothing but dying grass and earth. He started to say something but only shook his head and led them out into the field.

What was going on? they wondered, watching him standing in the clearing between the two roads. What is going on?

All of this nonverbal communication was of much interest to Ed Carmel. At the time, he and Peter both worked as attendant nurses at Boston State Hospital's drug-addiction unit. Ed had, in the weeks preceding the trip to Maine, learned a great deal about Peter. In particular, Ed was puzzled by the narrow determination of this person who had recently returned from a year in VISTA and was biding his time at the hospital, waiting to be drafted. The way he talked about it, it sounded as if Peter *wanted* to be a soldier. He even talked of enlisting! In 1966, when the U.S. was pouring troops into Southeast Asia like ants! It didn't make sense.

Ed hoped that Peter might get some insights into some of the things that were going on inside his head, things about the military or his parents that he was blocking. Once, after Peter and Ed had smoked a joint together, Ed put on a record of Laura Huxley reading poetry. "Turn it off!" Peter shouted. "Turn it off! It sounds like my mother!" Peter was blocking a lot of feelings.

As the group emerged from the cabin periodically that weekend to walk around Orgonon, Ed wondered if their talks would ever get to the point where they could talk about some of the things they were all feeling about Orgonon. Including Peter.

"Peeps, I know it was difficult for you when Mummy left. It was difficult for all of us. I have told you many times that people are afraid of my work. That is why they all left."

They all left. Maybe that was a whole bad thing. It was different after Oranur because no one laughed any more and one by one they left. I started to smile. I always wanted to smile when it got serious.

"Peeps, don't run away. This is very serious. It is going to get very tough. Many people have run away. Even Mummy. But she came back. It is very difficult for her. Do you understand? It's okay, you can cry. Go ahead. Cry."

He always wanted me to understand everything and I had to because no one else would but I didn't understand why he had to yell at Mummy or why the tears from one eye hit the lady on the head and the tears from the other eye went into the writing and made the page wrinkly.

"Look at me, Peeps," he said, and held his arms around me until I cried. He was sad too and I loved him too. It was so sad when the lab was empty and Mummy and Daddy fought. I wanted them to be happy. He touched my hair and his hand felt good.

"But Daddy, why does everyone run away?"

"Because they are afraid of the work, Peter. Many people became afraid when the attacks started but everyone was afraid after Oranur because the Oranur experiment showed them how powerful Orgone Energy really is. All the people who were saying they believed and understood really didn't. When they saw the truth of it in the experiment, they all ran away. Truth is very powerful, Peeps, I know."

"What is going to happen?"

"I don't know. I just don't know what will happen. I am convinced that someone in the government knows how important this work is. I think President Eisenhower is the kind of person who would help us, but he may not be able to actually come out and help. I don't know. I think there is going to be a big battle, but we must be brave."

"But why is it a battle?"

He squeezed me and looked into the fire. The flames were pretty. They were in the window too, but if I opened the window they would be gone. I wondered if the hole in the snow would still be warm in the morning.

"It is a battle because I have discovered the Life Energy, Peeps. Orgonomy provides a whole new way of freeing man from the emotional armor he has worn for centuries. But mankind has learned to hate what it loves. Men do not want to be free or healthy, so they attack anybody who says that man can be free and happy. It is an emotional plague that is attacking me, and it is deadly. That is why people are running away. They are afraid."

"Are you afraid?"

"Yes, of course."

They were sitting in the cabin in front of the fire when the October sun broke through the clouds and sparkled on the dying grass. Peter jumped up and said, "Come on, come on. I want to show you something," and they trooped out of the cabin and made their way once again up the long hill to the observatory.

It had rained and they had been cramped inside the cabin for a long time, so it was good to get out and walk vigorously. At the top of the hill they stopped and pressed cupped hands to the observatory's big picture windows. It was strange for Ed to find Reich's working place so closed. He would have thought it would be open, welcoming and alive. Yet even if he had come in summer, he might have found many museum goers coming away confused, feeling as if the museum had no point to it. But here, in the fall, he could look through the reflection of lovely leaves on the big windows inside to the red linoleum floor with rugs and furniture neatly arranged. There were paintings on the wall, many of naked women. Two paintings in particular caught Ed's eye. One was a picture of a man or a woman holding a child in front of a burning building. He wondered if it reflected some incident in Reich's life, a tragedy, perhaps. On the other side of the room, hanging over a huge stone fireplace, was another fire picture. This one showed a person sitting in profile in front of a fire. It was hard to tell if it was a man or a woman. He wanted to ask Peter about the fire paintings, but all morning long Peter had been avoiding questions.

As they slowly moved off the porch, he wondered why Peter

had brought them up here again, why he had been so anxious to show them this. Was this what he wanted them to see? The emptiness? Was that what Peter felt? Ed's reflections were interrupted by Peter's voice, more excited now, saying, "Come on, come on." He led them off the road into the woods.

In glaring October sunshine they followed his voice into the woods, losing sight of each other among swatting swinging branches and spider webs. When the branches stopped flying into him, Ed stopped and looked around. They were standing in the middle of an old dump. Tin cans, old beer cans, glass bottles, old pots, even a broken toilet seat seemed to rise and fall out of the soft brown ground. The others knelt down, pulling away the pine-needled skin of earth and roots. They picked up glasses and bottles of all sizes and shapes. Peter danced around through the broken glass scattering bits of sunlight, his feet occasionally sinking into the thin veil of moss and needles. "This is what I wanted to show you," he said. "This is what I wanted to show you!"

It gave Ed goose bumps. What was Peter afraid of? Why had he brought them here to this old dump? Did he understand what he was communicating to them? Ed picked up an old porcelain basin and turned it over and over in his hands. A few others had picked up blue Phillip's Milk of Magnesia bottles and held them up to the sun.

Crunching over the top of the dump, Peter danced over to Ed and smiled. "Hey. Isn't this neat? I bet we could find some really great old bottles if we dug around."

"Is that all?" asked Ed.

Peter looked at him. "What do you mean?" He shrugged and crunched back over the top of the dump.

Outside, it was getting dark. It was so quiet I could almost hear the wind coming off the top of Saddleback, far away. But the only noise near me was dry empty branches in the birch tree by the steps to the observatory.

I buckled on my skis in front of the observatory on the shiny crusted snow. The skis made a scratchy noise until I put them in the path Mummy and I made with the sled. Then I skied down the hill quickly.

Once I almost fell. If I hurt myself it would be the third bad thing. Oranur was the first and the FDA was the second and I wanted the third one to come before Christmas. The FDA were quacks who said the accumulator was bad and that Daddy couldn't let people use it any more. The FDA made people scared too.

I waited for Daddy at the turnoff to the lower cabin. A few snowflakes started to fall making it even quieter. The skis slipped over the powdery crust. The sound of light snow falling in just darkness was quieter than no snow at all and after a while the noise of Daddy's car came down the hill. I waved to him as he passed me and skied fast on the dusty red swirling snow all the way home. If I fell it would be the third bad thing.

Back in the cabin that evening they all sat around the fireplace and watched the flames, nursing strong tea laced with brandy and garnished with flakes of marijuana. There was little talking any more; people were exhausted not only from the tension around Orgonon but from the tensions that come when catharsis or expansion doesn't. They had been together for nearly three days in this strange energy capitol and their own reserves were dwindling.

Soaring in the back of their minds was the question of energy, always the energy that seemed to be everywhere. When they had come back to the cabin and started the fire, Ed had noticed that the rock fireplace was painted grey. When he asked Peter d'Errico about the paint, he learned that Dr. Reich had the rocks painted grey because he felt that they too exuded this bad energy. Ed sipped his tea thoughtfully. He had heard discussions about Reich's later years. The notion of Orgone Energy as he understood it seemed dynamic and exciting. What had gone wrong? What did this place do to Reich, his followers and his family? He thought about the painting in the observatory, the one of the burning building, and wondered what it symbolized.

A gust of wind blew some branches against the side of the building and the sudden noise made everyone jump with fear. Was it a ghost? Ed decided to try to talk to Peter. He began slowly.

"Peter, I know it must be difficult for you to talk about a lot of stuff. But you know, we are all here together and we are all feeling very uptight about the things we don't understand about your father. It would help us if you could explain, even a little bit, about how you feel about this place. It is very confusing for us. . . ."

Peter hesitated. "What do you want me to tell you about?" His voice sounded defensive.

"Could you tell us about the fear? We all feel it."

Peter watched the fire for a long time before he answered. The flames reflected in his eyeglasses.

"It is very hard to explain," he began slowly. "There is this fear that comes when people deal with my father. I'm not saying this place is haunted or anything, it is just that strange things happen to people when they come in contact with the work."

"Do you understand what it is? Could you tell us about it?"

"I guess . . . I guess a lot of it has to do with the sort of cosmic nature of the work. It was so far ahead, so revolutionary, that people are afraid. . . ."

"That's just it," Ed said earnestly, "that fear. It might be easier to understand if you could tell us what you are afraid of."

"What do you mean?"

Ed had tried once before to talk with Peter about his feelings, but he always seemed to say what he felt he ought to say. He seemed blocked from his own feelings. "You are always talking about what others are afraid of. But now we are the others and we are here with you. Maybe we could understand what we are afraid of here if you could tell us what you are afraid of."

Again for a long time, Peter was still. He drank some tea and shook his head. "Well, I don't know. There are good things and bad things and I guess I really don't understand them all. Like I'm afraid of monsters in the water." He grinned and shook his head. Then he was serious again. "There were some really bad things. . . . Like I showed you bullet holes where people just came up and shot at our sign. I had to wear a whistle around my neck because my father was afraid something might happen to me."

"What? Did anything ever happen? Was someone going to get you or something?"

Peter turned pale. He finished his tea and put the cup on the floor. "I . . . I really can't say. It is so confusing. I don't know if you'd even believe half the stuff that happened. It sounds so incredible. I mean you've already seen the cloudbusters and stuff but it is so . . . so open-ended, I really don't know where to begin.

"When I was in France, taking my junior year abroad—funny, it was in October too, in 1963—I had a motorcycle accident. Dislocated my right shoulder. I had to have gas three times because they had such a hard time getting my shoulder back in. Each time I went under the gas I had the same dream. The amazing thing about this dream was that I was sure I had had it before. The dream was that there were two realities in my life and they were not parallel. They would meet somewhere, sometime, and it would be very scary. That motorcycle accident still haunts me, like the motorcycles in Cocteau's *Orpheus*. I'm afraid

I'm going to bump into that other dream sometime. Maybe the bad things are in that other dream and I am so afraid of them I can't remember them. Maybe in a few years. I'm much more sure of the good things."

There was silence again. Ed wondered if Peter would ever find out how the two realities came together. Did he know how many realities there were to sort out? Mother-Father, Mother-Son, Father-Son, dream-reality. Ed said, "Why don't you tell us some of the nice things?"

Peter looked at the fire. "Gee, it has been such a long time since I talked about it. There were a lot of really nice things. I really think I had a great childhood." He thought for a while, and then he spoke again. "Fire. Fires were nice things. In winter, life seemed to revolve around fire. I'd come home from school at night with a Hardy Boys mystery and a bag of King Cole Potato Chips and a Pepsi and finish all three in one sitting in front of the fireplace.

"I used to have a special game with the fire where I'd take a marble and clear a path into the coals underneath the burning logs and roll a marble in. After a few minutes, I'd roll it back out and drop it into a glass of water and watch it crack. They never broke and they were so beautiful. . . ."

As Peter talked about fire, the fire was reflected in his glasses. It gave Ed the sinking feeling in his stomach that he got when he talked to schizophrenic patients at the hospital. There was a transition point that seemed to come in their talking when in the middle of a conversation they jumped to a different level. They could be talking about a TV show or a ball game and suddenly all the pattern of thought and speech, both conscious and unconscious, merged and they were communicating on two levels. One might start out talking about A and then drift onto B. Then after a while, C would emerge, and C might actually be a statement about the nature of A. The psychologist, Ed felt, had somehow to help the patient understand the basic pattern of his thinking and learn to read its message. But it was hard. You couldn't tell, you had to show. He knew Peter's father had been one of the first to understand that, and here Peter was sitting in his father's house talking about fire and telling how much he loved it. All weekend long he had been telling them, nonverbally, that he was terrified of fire.

Every time they built a fire he ran over every five minutes to make sure no coals got on the floor; he worried about the oil burner overheating and talked about chimney fires. There were fire extinguishers everywhere and surrounding the stoves were thick asbestos panels. And in the observatory, on the wall opposite the huge stone fireplace, were the paintings: a person holding a child in front of a fire, a solitary figure before a fire. When Peter finished talking, Ed asked, "What did your father think about fire?"

Peter didn't hesitate. "He always said the only color an artist couldn't capture was that of a dying fire."

After dinner I wanted to surprise Mummy so I said I would do the dishes and she could dry.

She and Daddy were talking and I wanted them to talk a lot together and be happy so I washed the dishes slowly.

When I was through washing they were still talking so I started to dry. Mummy said, "Are you ready for me to come and dry?"

"Not yet," I said, and turned on some water to make it sound like I was still washing. It made me happy to hear them talking together.

The silverware made a lot of noise so I had to do it piece by piece. It must have been quiet because Mummy said, "Are you sure you don't want me to come in and dry yet?"

"Nope, still not done." I tried to keep from smiling but I did. They didn't see me smile though because I turned away quick.

It made me feel good to see them sitting together by the fire, talking. The fire made them look warm.

Finally, when I was done I said, "Okay, You can come now." And when she saw that the dishes were all dried she was so surprised she hugged me. By the fire, Daddy was smiling. I felt good so I decided to go out and play in the new snow.

The snow was light and powdery falling out of the sky. I walked away from the house so I wouldn't break the crust and then I knelt down and used my hand like a saw to cut a round hole out of the crust. It didn't break. It came out perfectly round, so maybe the third bad thing wouldn't come at all and we could all not worry and be happy. I lifted the circle of snow crust out like a manhole cover and licked snow off the bottom where it is best. I wondered if there were still coals glowing up on the hill where Tom and I burned the brush.

The fire was dying.

Ed looked around the room and saw that a couple of people had fallen asleep. He realized it was very late. "Shall we stop?" he asked.

Peter was leaning forward, staring into the fire. He shook his head. Peter d'Errico leaned toward Peter and said, "Are you sure you want to go on?"

Peter nodded. "Snow," he said. There was a long silence. Someone put a new log on the fire and they watched the flames lick at it. "Snow was really something up here in winter. You should really come up here sometime and see Orgonon when there is snow all over everything. Tom used to take his shovel and cut huge tunnels in snowbanks for me and Kathy to play in. I spent a lot of time with Tom. We used to cut brush together and make big fires in the snow. That ax handle right there that we use for a fire poker came off one of his old axes. He gave me one so I could help him. We had a lot of fun with the axes. I remember once we spent a long time cutting brush and burning it and then that night I went outside and started digging a tunnel under the crust."

I raked the dry grainy snow out from the hole and when I had a big pile I pushed it away.

I did that for a long time with new snow falling on my face, licking at it and pulling more and more snow out of the hole. When the hole was deep enough so I could almost get in it, I put my head inside. It was dark and little grains of dry snow made falling noises as the sides of the tunnel caved in slowly.

I ran inside to get a flashlight and propped it up in the snow so it was shining into the tunnel. Soon it was so long I had to get inside to keep digging. But I still had to be careful or the crust might break.

After a while it was a regular cave. It was like a little house. The flashlight on the crust made it look like millions of diamonds in a snow palace. I pretended it was a long palace dance hall and Daddy and I were dancing with Mummy in a pretty white slip and the three of us danced around and around and we were all happy. I was so happy I wanted to show them the snow cave. Very carefully I crawled out and ran inside. "Mummy, Daddy, come and look at the house I made in the snow! Come and look!"

"There was an incredible crust on the snow that day. It was so thick you could walk on it. After dinner, in the dark, I went outside and started digging a tunnel underneath the crust. The walls inside were soft snow. I ran back into the house to get a flashlight to help me dig and that is why I remember it. It was beautiful inside that white snow tunnel with sparkling cold walls of snow sliding around me as I scooped it out. Then I remember

I heard a noise outside. It was snowing and underneath the light over the door I could see my father and mother standing in the doorway watching me and laughing. I just think that is one of the nicest memories I have, of being in that hole and seeing my mother and father laughing at the way I must have looked to them."

I ran out ahead of them and crawled into the little snow house with the flashlight. When I got all the way inside I went all the way to the end of the tunnel and turned around slowly so that I could look out the round castle doorway and see the circle of light at the real door where Mummy and Daddy were standing in the doorway laughing. We were happy again together. It was snowing harder already and I had to squint to see them in between all the thousands of white snowflakes and I saw that Mummy had stopped laughing. She watched the snow fall and she looked very sad.

In the middle of a sentence, Peter suddenly stopped talking. He stared into the fire. For a moment Ed thought he could feel Peter's mind stumbling around in open darkness. After a few moments of silence, Peter stood up. He turned and walked quickly into the large dark bedroom that had been his parents' and in a few minutes they heard him crying.

When he returned a while later, he went to a bookshelf and came back with a book. He sat down in front of the book. "I want to read you a story," he said.

He began reading. It was a children's story about knights living in a castle. The special thing about these knights was that the bravest of all knights had a shining star in their shields. At the time of the story, however, there was no knight who had a star. A war came and the knights went off to fight the giants. The youngest knight, much to his distress, was left to guard the castle. He really wanted to go and fight, to win a star, but he knew his duty and stayed at the castle. While the knights were in battle, three giants came in disguises and tried to enter the castle but the youngest knight, Sir Roland, obeyed the orders and refused to let them in.

Soon the knights returned to the castle, victorious. They went into a great hall

"... and Sir Roland came forward with the key of the gate, to give his account of what he had done in the place to which the commander had appointed him. The lord of the castle bowed to him as a sign for him to begin, and just as he opened his mouth to speak, one of the knights cried out:

"'The shield! The shield! Sir Roland's shield!'

"Everyone turned to look at the shield that Sir Roland carried on his left arm. He himself could see only the top of it, and did not know what they could mean. But what they saw was the golden star of knighthood, shining brightly from the center of Sir Roland's shield. There had never been such amazement in the castle before.

"Sir Roland knelt before the lord of the castle to receive his commands. He still did not know why everyone was looking at him so excitedly.

"'Speak, Sir Knight,' said the commander, as soon as he could find his voice after his surprise, 'and tell us all that has happened today at the castle. Have you been attacked? Have any giants come hither? Did you fight them alone?'

"'No, my lord,' said Sir Roland. 'Only one giant has been here and he went away silently when he found he could not enter.'

"Then he told all that had happened through the day.

"When he finished, the knights all looked at one another but no one spoke a word. Then they looked again at Sir Roland's shield to make sure that their eyes had not deceived them, and there the golden star was still shining.

"After a little silence, the lord of the castle spoke.

"'Men make mistakes,' he said, 'but our silver shields are never mistaken. Sir Roland has fought and won the hardest battle of all today.'

"Then all the others rose and saluted Sir Roland, who was the youngest knight that ever carried the golden star."

When he finished reading the story, Peter looked up. He closed the storybook and put it away. They were all silent, watching the last coals of the fire glimmer and glow.

To Ed, it was a simple, gracious way for Peter to explain what had happened. His father's world was still locked away inside him; he was a kind of young soldier, guarding a mystery that nobody seemed to understand. Ed did not know why Peter had cried; perhaps their questioning had been the giant, perhaps Peter felt himself wavering. But in the end, he had guarded successfully. He was the knight. His childhood was running through him as if on some private projector, impenetrable, private, guarded. It had almost broken through, but something held it back. Ed wondered what it would take to break Peter's shield.

The next morning they all left Orgonon early. From the observatory, Tom watched their cars pull out of the driveway. It had just begun to snow, which was not that unusual for October, and the thin flakes were like a veil between him and the tiny cars slowly turning out of the driveway. Tom watched the cars leave and then he watched the gentle snow falling. It fell on the bright leaves that still clung to the trees. At the other end of the path, light grains of snow tumbled and fell down the dark-brown crevices in the bust. In the forest, it would have made a light noise coming through the branches. Tom sat by the window for a long time and then he stood up. It was time to sharpen his ax and varnish his snowshoes.

Chapter 5

ASA
NISI
MASA
—The magic words from Fellini's 8½

Coming home!

To make a movie!

Beep! Beep! Canoers paddling down the mighty Androscoggin River wave as my trusty blue VW cruises up Route 16 toward Rangeley, a hand waving out of the sunroof.

Coming home! The moon's crescent hangs onto the afternoon as if it is going to slip off the day and fall down with all the blinking strawberry blossom stars along the shoulder of this road that takes me home.

To make a movie! Already my eye is the camera and photographs rear up at me with each turn of the road: Along the river, heavy old pilings from lumber days rest on the reflection of frail reeds. They glisten with moss. In places, the river splits, yawns slowly past an island, and closes up again with a string of bubbles. It is exciting to be in a movie about my father. A real movie! And I'm in it! I've got all kinds of ideas to tell the director, a Yugoslav named Makavejev, and I wish he could have his movie camera right here for this road.

Zooming into back country now, past Thirteen-Mile Wood, the ribbon road bounces up over a thank-you-ma'am and the VW enters a straightaway, a great green channel of birch trees just glowing in the afternoon sun. A perfect day to come home. I haven't been back since that weekend, that crazy weekend in 1966. I've been in the Army, and worked for a newspaper. And now I'm going to be in this movie.

In the background, rich hazy mountains loom up, shadowed by thunderclouds over Mooselucmeguntic Lake and the Rangeley Lakes. The movie crew will be coming today or tomorrow. Too bad it is June, and not July, when the flowers are better. I told Makavejev when he was here in the fall that the flowers are best in July. That was when I first met him, in the fall of '69.

Dusan Makavejev, the Yugoslav film director, came to the United States to explore the possibilities of a film that would capture some of Reich's ideas on film. We met once or twice and he invited me to screenings of two earlier films, *Love Affair, or The Case of the Missing Switchboard Operator*, and *Innocence Unprotected*. The way he mingled fiction and documentary, as if he always wanted to remind the audience that they were watching a movie, was great and the prospect of being in a movie like that really turned me on.

I was glad when Makavejev telephoned me the night before he was to return to Europe to seek additional financial aid for the film. He said he wanted to talk with me again. At the time, in the fall of 1969, I was an editor at the Staten Island *Advance* and told him I could finish work by 10 P.M. if he wanted to take the Staten Island Ferry over from Manhattan.

A little after 10 he bounced into the city room wearing soft European clothing and grinning through his beard. As we drove to my small cottage in South Beach, in the shadow of the Verrazano Narrows Bridge, I told him about Staten Island's largely conservative population and apologized for its remoteness.

"No, no," Makavejev protested, waving his hands in the air, "I love the people on Staten Island. In Manhattan the people are always walking around looking angry at each other as if they want to fight. But they never speak a word. They just look angry. Here, I come off the ferry onto Staten Island and I see two people yelling at each other! Looking at each other and yelling! It was wonderful!"

He flipped through a stack of my photographs while I prepared two huge helpings of bacon, eggs, and home fries and a pot of coffee.

While we ate, Makavejev talked about my father, but I was really interested in talking about movies. Since that crazy weekend in 1966, I had thought little about my childhood. It was safer to go to science-fiction movies where there were happy endings. When I met Makavejev I had been out of the Army barely a year and was working at becoming a journalist. Besides, my father's name was still regarded as a joke in most places except Europe, where radical students had discovered his early political work. I was ignorant of most of his work in politics, sociology, and psychology. I was into media.

Makavejev told me how as a student in Belgrade he had discovered Reich's work and felt it was terribly important. He told me that in 1938 a Yugoslav was imprisoned for reading Reich.

Like most Europeans who were familiar with Reich, Makavejev was especially interested in the early political writings. He said he felt that Reich had looked at politics creatively and that what he wanted to do was see the same way only with a camera, visually. "When society is alive and healthy, there are snake dances in the streets," he said, snaking his hands through the air, "and you can see just by looking at the shoes that there are many different people. But when society is repressive you only see identical boots, marching in rigid lines."

By the time we finished our coffee, it was nearly midnight. We were still talking, so we went down to the South Beach boardwalk and walked up and down watching the sparkling lights of Brooklyn and Coney Island reflecting off the bay.

Jokingly, I told him that only a few months before, I had "guarded" that same beach, a few hundred yards up, at Fort Wadsworth, the small Army post that lurked beneath the Verrazano Narrows Bridge.

He didn't believe me.

"Yup. I was a real soldier."

He asked me about my life and I told him what I had done. "After college I spent a year in VISTA—the domestic peace corps —and then I decided I was sick of draft-dodging and wanted to work for a newspaper. So I decided to let myself be drafted and worked in a drug-addiction rehabilitation center in Boston for a few months until I got my greetings. After Basic Training at Fort Jackson, South Carolina, I spent my whole tour at Fort Wadsworth, right up there, first as a key-punch operator and then as a public-information specialist. I did articles and took photographs and wrote speeches for the generals and colonels. For the last eleven months of my tour, I worked part-time evenings at the *Advance* and went full time when I got out. Just a few weeks ago I was promoted to copy editor."

"And your father's work?" asked Makavejev. "You aren't interested? You have feelings?" He held his hand up and turned it from side to side, smiling, leaving it open.

I didn't know what to say. It *was* open. I hadn't given it much thought. "I guess I've been trying to live my own life," I said. "I guess I'm thinking about a career in journalism. I took a month's leave of absence this summer to do some writing. Maybe I'll quit and write a book or something. But I'm not involved in carrying out his work, if that is what you mean. He always told me to live my own life."

"Maybe if you have quit when I come back with the movie

crew you could come to Maine with us. You could help, perhaps, telling about visual things."

"Yeah," I said, "I'd like that."

Driving back to Manhattan, Makavejev talked about his films, his family, his politics, and his plans. If all went well, he said, he would return in midwinter or at least by spring to begin shooting. Yes, it would be a sort of documentary but well, there might be some fiction. He wasn't sure. The best he could say, as we drove up the West Side Highway past a darkened Manhattan, was that it would be a film "inspired by Reich."

Parked in front of his hotel, we talked more. He asked about Orgonon. Pleased by someone's interest in that place that had been so quiet in my mind for so long, I talked.

"Well, there are lots of flowers. The best time to start would be around the Fourth of July because the place is mad with daisies and Indian paintbrushes. Thick flowers. On some fields it looks as if there is nothing but a blanket of red and white. It shines when the wind rolls over it. You could get great shots just panning the camera around in those back fields where we used to go for walks together. If you could get it at dusk. Dusk is great. Even after the sun goes down this soft green-golden light hangs over the fields like magic and after it is dark, the new tips of the fir trees glow in the dark. And when evening winds come up, it becomes all blurry."

"And do you have a bust of Reich?"

"Yes. There is a bust in the lower cabin—that is the cabin that is in my name—and there's one on the tomb as well."

"Perhaps we could do something with a double image, using the bust. . . ."

"Yeah," I cut in, imagination racing, electrified by the idea of others seeing all those things in a real movie, a movie that was already going on in my head. "Yeah, another possibility is the lake. The lake, first thing in the morning with mist rising off it.

You saw a picture of it in that stack I showed you at my house. It would be great to have a scene on this misty lake and then right beneath the surface of the lake or even on the surface, yeah, on the surface, floating right across the top of the lake without even making a ripple, sailing through the mist toward the camera comes the bust of Reich!"

Makavejev sat up. "Yes. Perhaps with a boat or a raft. . . ."

We threw out ideas faster and faster until we were yelling at each other. The movie seemed like a great catalyst, reminding me of scenes and things I had not remembered for years. Makavejev, of course, was interested in practical and immediate information. He called it "informations."

"Tell me," he said. "In winter. Could we get there in winter?"

"Winter. Wow. Sure. My cabin is winterized. We used to live there. But of course the observatory is closed. It is a museum, you know. You'd have to contact the trust fund about that. But you could still walk around on snowshoes and see it. Of course, the water is off. But there are motels. And some great scenes. When it rains and freezes it makes an incredible crust and whole fields are like huge unbroken pages of snow. Huge white football pads of snow on trees, scrimmaging the wind. The wind is a whole nother thing, coming over the mountains and across the lake. . . . The lake . . . why sure! The lake!"

The whole picture slid into my mind as if someone had turned on a projector.

"Hey! Listen to this! You start the movie in winter, with the movie crew struggling down from the cabin in the wind, trying to get to the lake. Lots of wind, yelling and tromping around through the snow. The movie crew finally gets to the lake and of course it is frozen. Everything is frozen at the beginning. But they have to get to water, right? You need to get the lake. So with snow and wind flurrying all around they start chopping away, with pickaxes and axes. As they chop, all overexposed with steamy breath and grunting ice, the camera pans away. Down the shore, swinging his ax against alder, cleaning out the scrub brush, is Tom. Tom! Burning the branches. Making a cloud of white smoke. Then you pick up on Tom and make the whole movie from his angle, going into the whole story about Reich from Tom's point of view. . . ."

What a great movie! I could hardly wait.

All winter I waited to hear from Makavejev. He finally arrived in May 1970 and after shooting some interviews in New York was going to be in Rangeley now, the first week in June. I had quit my job. I didn't know what would happen. Makavejev even said he might do a scene of me and Tom together. It would be great to have a scene with me and Tom in this movie.

Driving up the last stretch of Badger Road before the cabin turnoff, late afternoon shadows ragged across the fields, I see Tom, a lone figure pushing his lawnmower over the lawns in front of the lab. He's already had supper and come back to finish the mowing. I beep and wave going down the drive. I'm anxious to open the cabin. Windows and doors flung open, old dark winter air rushes out into the evening. The water has not been turned on, so I grab a pail and head to the lake. At dusk, I am mopping the cabin floor with cold lake water, getting ready for the movie.

Shimmering, vibrating in the invisible leaves of heat. All the way around the sunny, hot field.

Tom steered the tractor in square circles and behind us the grass fell back in the tractor's noise, lay straight, turned yellow, and made a sweet smell.

I hung onto the grey fender and watched Tom bounce on the seat waiting for him to stop the tractor and let me drive. He promised. And then later Daddy said we could do stuff together.

All around us the trees that ran along the hospital field's stone fences moved past slowly poking into the bright sky. If I closed my eyes tight all of a sudden the place where the trees were stayed white hot behind my eyes and the sky turned dark. It was like a reflection.

Once Mummy and I were rowing in the lake and two men came by in a boat and said have you seen a dead deer floating around in the water? They said they had shot him and tracked him to the lake but he disappeared. They thought he had drowned and was floating somewhere just beneath the surface. We said no, but I was scared that I would see it brown and dead in the water and that my feet would touch it.

Rowing is okay but I don't like swimming that much. I get scared swimming at our dock because I can't see bottom. There are ants and big spiders between the boards and there may be a dead deer floating around somewhere. Tom taught me how to swim up at Quimby Pond where the water is shallow for a long ways out and Tom came over and said ain't you learned to swim yet? I said no and he picked me up and just threw me into the water. When I came up I said, "Gee, Tom, I dwownded!" He always tells me that story. Now I can dive pretty good when I go swimming at the town dock. It isn't as scary there. I have to stand on the dock for a long time holding my hands out in front of me but I can do it. When I dive it is just like when the mower blade dives into the grass after we lift it over a rock. It is funny the way Donald Duck dives because he holds his hands in front of his face like he is praying. Maybe he is afraid too. I tried diving like that once but I got water in my nose. Some of the boys wear ear plugs and nose plugs but I don't dive that deep because they say there is a pipe in the deep part, sticking up, and if you dive on it it will drill a hole through your head and kill you. There is a special way of shaking your head sideways to make water in your ears come out and when it comes out it is hot like the sun was in my head. Once I asked Daddy if there was a place in the sky where the sky is what is hard and the place where trees are is all wind, an upside-down world like when I close my eyes on the tractor. He said it was a good question.

Tom leaned back and yelled, "You see that over there?" He pointed to a big place in the grass we hadn't mowed where it was all matted down.

"That's where a deer been sleepin'. They leave the grass all pressed down like that."

I looked at it as we drove past. The grass was pressed down. It was like a place where someone had slept.

"She must have been a pretty big one," said Tom.

The circles got smaller and smaller like the field was a big box and we were unwinding it going around and around making hay. Down across the road the pond sparkled in the sunlight. Sometimes there was a black speck that was a boat with fishermen or maybe the hunters looking for the deer.

When Tom takes us swimming over to Quimby Pond we have to dodge cowpies and thistles in the pasture to get over to the shore. Coming back across I always look up the road to the house where that girl and her mother lived. They came here one summer and invited me over a lot. It was a funny house because the kitchen sink was black and water drops looked silvery in it. One day I was there and the girl said do you want to play doctor. I said okay. We went up to her bedroom and closed the door. She got undressed and then I got undressed. She had breasts that moved smoothly in the light. When she lay down they went away except for the darker part. And there was hair between her legs that I don't have. When it was my turn to lie down her fingers touched my legs like grass when I run naked in the trees. When I went downstairs her mother was at the sink working the pump. Water was coming out and swirling in the flat black sink. She said, "You'll come and visit again, won't you?" Tom takes us to Quimby Pond a lot. The water isn't deep at all and there is foam at the place where the pasture meets the water.

When we came around again, Tom shook his head and said, "See right there." He pointed to the place where the deer slept. It disappeared under the cutter blade. "She sure was a big one," said Tom.

Tom always calls things she, but I can't tell how he knows. He says I guess she'll rain today or I guess she'll be a hot one. Or when I'm oiling the mower blade he says, "You got her yet?"

"Hey Tom," I said. "Do you suppose she needs gas?" We had gone around the field in square circles many times.

"Oh, in a little while, I guess."

Grasshoppers raced us across the field.

Tom's mower woke me up before sunrise: he was out mowing in the grainy morning light, walking near the lab with oil smoke from the old mower hanging in a low blue cloud over the dark dew-hung grass.

I wished Makavejev could get that on film, and was anxious to discuss it with him. I still wasn't sure how he wanted to use me in the movie. The arrangement was that he would come over to the cabin sometime, perhaps in the evening.

The noise from Tom's mower followed me around the cabin as I fixed breakfast and put on my work clothes. My mower, a bright-red one that I bought the year before, was in the garage. It started up quickly and we began mowing in long straight swaths across the yard. It would have been great to have Makavejev come down, cameras whirring, and catch me doing the same thing Tom was doing up the road.

But they didn't come.

After a while I went up to the lab looking for Tom but he was gone too. Looking through the windows, I could smell the way it was even though the windows were tightly shut: a combination of cold concrete and the liquids of science. The sound of instruments at rest, the smell of hot glass all mixed with cool air.

Through the windows, it looked cold and barren. The tables were yellowed and cracked. Chairs and boxes stood around just where they had stood for the last thirteen years, as if someone suddenly walked out and left everything. The very first cloudbuster, a fabrication of wood and metal pipes, stood in one corner next to a sink with jars, glass bottles with glass tubing. My father wanted it for a museum. Maybe someday it would be in one. At the next window, I was looking into a room lined with shelves holding rocks, bits of wood, more jars, and crumbled wrinkled cards and notes tacked to the wall. The light was diffused and showed me instruments and cobwebs, dust and black lichen on the floor, arranged like shadows of the people who were no longer there.

All around the back of the lab, the concrete pilings had rotted and were decaying, falling into rubble on the ground. In places the building had shifted and a section of lab clung to a piling by fractions of an inch, as if the whole thing would sigh in a heavy wind and sink slowly around the pillar.

I walked around the sagging barn and shed. It was all locked and closed, cobwebbed and dusty. Only the lawns were open. It didn't really bother me that the estate was closed to me. The management of the estate was carried on by the trustee in a very independent manner. Perhaps it was just as well that I was not involved in my father's affairs. I had to live my own life.

But I was in the movie. Makavejev told me I was, and I wondered where he was. Walking out over the smooth green grass I went to the apple tree where Daddy took movies of me and my mother picking apples. I stood right in the same place where I stood naked in that other movie that he made, laughing and clowning, picking up apples.

Just beyond the apple tree I could make out the faint outline of a large rectangle in the grass. This was what I wanted Makavejev to see. You see, my father bought Orgonon from Tom's grandfather. Tom grew up at Orgonon. When he was a kid he used to bring cattle in for milking from pastures that are now the forests he cares for. So the movie should have that too, Tom, perpetually working on this land.

Imperceptibly at first, and then more and more distinctly, outlines of buildings that once dotted his grandfather's farm show through the cropped grass. Tom stops where the old forge was and picks bits of iron and slag from the earth. He mows carefully around the cloudbuster platform which stands on the imprint of the old barn's foundations.

No doubt there existed somewhere, in an attic or antique store, an old daguerreotype or glass-plate negative of Jesse Ross himself, proprietor of the farm on Dodge Pond. In this photograph, Jesse Ross would have held himself proudly, in his best store-bought clothing, putting forth the best image he could muster of himself as a landowner for the gaze of all future viewers.

He would have had no inkling that a hundred years later the same box that froze his image would have developed so that it could make the images move, come to life in such a way that had he wished he could have made a movie of his grandson Tom. Tom the child bringing cows into the barn. Tom working for The Doctor, tearing the same barn down. Tom building a platform for a strange machine over the very same spot and then mowing around and around the same grass, mowing with his, Jess Ross's, great-great-grandson so that, in all, five generations would have put their sweat into the same land.

Now that was a movie!

I turned back toward the cabin to get my car. I was going to Rangeley to find Makavejev and talk to him about the movie.

Driving to town with Daddy, I reached into the glove compartment and took out the tire gauge. I flicked it and the measuring part slipped out to 23. That meant that scouts and Indians were alert within a 23-mile radius of the car. Looking out of the window, I could see them sitting on their ponies in the fields, watching us. They nodded as we drove past and I nodded back, smiling. It was good. They were watching.

I pushed the gauge back in and flicked it again. Thirty-three. They were at watch up to 33 miles away.

"What are you doing?" asked Daddy.

"Oh, this is how I tell my cavalry where to patrol and stuff."

"I see."

The road dipped down sharply making it look as if we were going to fall off a cliff right into the lake.

"Are they good soldiers?"

"Yup."

"Good."

The car slowed down at the turn and Rangeley Lake slid sideways off the window as we turned onto the main road. I checked the tire gauge.

"Peeps?"

"What?"

"Are you frightened?"

"A little bit, I guess. Are you?"

"Yes, somewhat."

At Doc Grant's we sat at our special table next to the stuffed deer and the setting sun came in through the screens so it rested on the deer's yellow-brown back.

Daddy looked at me for a long time because I was quiet. "Let's go home and call Mummy before we go to the movies," he said.

The sun on the deer's back was like the sun on the hay where the deer had slept. I closed my eyes when the mower came to cut the place where the deer had slept. When I put my hand on the deer's back, dust came up into the sun. The deer's nose was painted red and I felt around to see if I could find the bullet hole that killed him.

"Daddy," I said, "what is going to happen?"

Makavejev wasn't in town. I didn't know where he was. I worried. The movie had to be good. All those bad things that were scary in that night with Ed Carmel and those people that weekend, why am I thinking of them now? I want the movie to have good things, like Tom.

As long as I was in town, I went into Collins's to get some paint. Vernon Collins, the man who built Orgonon, still tends the store while his son, Elden, manages the firm.

Makavejev had been there already. He had spoken with Collins already.

"Yessir," said Vernon, "wasn't that something? I don't know if I'll live to see it but wasn't it something? Yessir. They come right in here with cameras and everything and asked me about the doctor. Yessir. Half the town knew about it and people was coming up to me and sayin', 'I hear you're a movie star.' Yessir, I don't know that it'll ever get over here. I told them that it was just going to be in Europe and if they wanted to go over there to see me, they was welcome to."

He picked a gallon can of creosote stain off one of the shelves and we walked back to the paint shaker.

"Yessir, he was a real nice fella. He spoke pretty good English too, even though there was a couple of them that didn't speak much English at all. Yessir, he asked me about the doctor and I told him that I'd been working with the doctor all along. Yessir, I told him that he was a good man to work for. Why, in all them years we worked together we never once had an argument. Yessir."

Screwing the can into the paint shaker, he flipped the switch and the can began its hard vibration. "Yessir. He asked me if folks in town was shy of the doctor and I said that a lot of people just didn't get to know him. Why, if there was a family burned out or something he was the first one to make a contribution. Yessir."

He looked out of the window for a while, shaking his head. "What you think of that storm on Saturday? Wasn't that something? Rain all day."

"Yeah, but we sure needed it."

"Oh, we needed the rain all right but gee whiz you couldn't go oudoahs. Nosir, there wasn't too much you could do. Yessir, we haven't had rain like that in a long time. Funny how rain seems to come just on days when you don't want it. Coss there's not much you can do about it." And then he added, "Since your dad died."

The paint shaker stopped with a thud, putting a new silence in the store. Vernon leaned down and unscrewed the creosote. Yessir. As we turned to walk back to the counter, a friend of Vernon's walking out of the store stopped and asked Vernon if he'd heard that Dr. Nile had died Saturday. They chatted for a minute about how he had been ailing for a while. Vernon was serious.

"How old you say he was?"

"He was seventy-six," answered the man.

"Is that all?" said Vernon, shaking his head. "Well, we all got to die sometime."

He carried the can of creosote back to the counter, walked around to the back, and pulled out the account book. "Yessir," he said, adding the cost of creosote and a pair of work gloves to our account.

"Yessir. You know, I was down at the University of Maine that time when they called him up, must have been back 1952 or 3 on account of that drought they was having."

"Yeah, I remember that, I was along and helped operate."

"Yessir. You know a lot of people laugh at that business with the cloudbusters, but I seen it work. Yessir."

"Yeah, I know what you mean. Those blueberry growers weren't really too sure it was going to work. But when it started raining the next day . . ."

"Yessir, it was really something to see. I remember one day I was drivin' around up near Orgonon with some friends and they seen the cloudbuster sitting there by the lab and they said, 'What's that?' and I told them about it but they just laughed so I said, 'Well, let's go up and see if the doctor is there and he can show you.' So we drove up and I went in and the doctor was there and I said, 'Doctor, I've got some friends down here who'd like to see the cloudbuster work,' and by gosh he come down and went up on the one right there by the laboratory and he said, 'Do you see that cloud right over there?' and pointed to a cloud up in the sky. Then he said, 'And do you see that one over there?' and pointed to another one. And then he started working and by gosh didn't those two clouds come right together into one big one. Yessir. And they just looked at it for a minute and the doctor said, 'Now watch,' and he started workin' on the cloudbuster again and in a couple of minutes that cloud opened up like a great big doughnut. Yessir."

I put the tire gauge back in the glove compartment and ran across the grass to the cloudbuster while Daddy parked the car. I started pulling the plugs and extending the pipes so by the time Daddy came to the platform I was finished and we stood quietly for a moment.

"Good," he said. "First let's feel what it is doing." We both looked at the sky and the mountains. It was warm. Afternoon clouds had already begun to bunch up on the mountains. With no wind at all, we could look down to the lake and see the clouds moving there, too. Up the road from the lake sunlight glowed on the new hay. Saddleback was purple, not blue like it should have been. The birds were quiet, hopping in the branches of the droopy birch next to the cloudbuster platform.

"Ahem, ahem," he said. "So. Let's start by working with the flow. The energy isn't moving at all. Start in the west and draw it over to the east."

I cranked the cloudbuster around, raising the pipes at the same time. Inside the base of the cloudbuster, gears clicked as it went around.

We started in the west because Orgone Energy flows from west to east and when we operate, it helps the flow. Daddy said never to draw from the east because that interrupts the streaming energy and causes storms.

The cloudbuster pipes moved around to the east, rubber plugs dangling.

"Good. All right. Come back now, slowly."

Creaking the wheels slower, I nursed the flow around to the south. I think the reason we go south is because south is warmer and if we went north we would get colder. But sometimes we go to the north too.

A car came up the road and we both stopped to look. It drove past and people looked out of the window. The car slowed down but kept on driving past us down toward Badger's Camps at the end of the road, with the people staring out of the window at us.

"Who was that?" asked Daddy.

"I don't know. . . ." It might have been spies. Sometimes Daddy had to chase agents and spies off Orgonon with a gun. There were all kinds of strange people coming and bothering him.

"It is okay, Peter. Let's continue. Bring it around again."

I raised the pipes, turned them around, and dropped them in the west. I held it for a minute to let the flow catch up and then started to swing around to the east again. It felt good cranking the cloudbuster around. That's why I like cloudbusting, because you feel better as the air gets better and you can go up, down, or sideways or any way it wants to go. There aren't any special rules.

"Okay. Now sweep the horizon. All the way around."

Cranking hard with both hands, I guided the pipes over the observatory hill and back down again, following the line of treetops all the way around to where it stops for the gap which is the tractor road out to the golden field of hay, and then on around.

"Ja. Now some more. Keep it going." Past the road, the lake, Saddleback, around the sky.

"You see, we are stroking it gently to get it moving again. When it moves, it is just like the streaming in your legs during treatment."

The gears made their dull, oily, metallic noise as we went around the hill once more, over the top of the observatory, back down again until the cloudbuster faced west, straight out through the opening in the trees to where the smooth grass had turned golden. We could smell it.

"Now. Zenith. All the way up."

He leaned back and looked straight up. I cranked the pipes straight up too until the little plugs hung straight down.

"Ja. Good. We'll leave it there for a while."

I came away from the controls and stood next to Daddy.

"I feel better," I said.

"Ja. It is better already. Look at the mountains."

Saddleback's purple was gone and it sparkled clear blue. It even looked closer to us. I felt better.

"Why are the streamings in my legs like the streamings in the sky?"

He smiled. "That is a good question. You see, Orgone Energy flows in your body the same way it flows in the atmosphere, or perhaps even in the universe. When I give you a treatment, I loosen up your body and get the energy streaming again."

"Why does it stop in the first place?"

"Well, sometimes I can see it when you have been playing with some of your friends. They have been brought up in an armored way, a way that makes them feel guilty when they touch their genitals, a way that makes them feel ashamed to cry. Some of that rubs off on you. It makes you tight and I have to loosen you up again."

"Why are they that way?"

"That's a question of history," he said, looking through his binoculars. "You see, most people have always thought that it is wrong to feel good and to feel happy. They are afraid of the good feelings, like the streamings. They try to stop these feelings in their children. They take their children and make them miserable. Well, if you take any natural drive and block it, it twists and turns but it still comes out. But instead of coming out in a straightforward, direct way, it comes out twisted and ugly. That is why some of your friends make dirty jokes about girls. They have learned to block their feelings, so they enjoy more the perverted, secondary feelings. When the blocking starts, their bellies get hard and their breathing becomes shallow. And they begin to hate."

"But my friends don't hate me."

"No, of course they don't. It isn't that kind of hate. It is a different, more subtle hatred. They put on a front of being nice and then the front becomes a real mask for the fear and hatred inside. They struggle to keep the good feelings down, inside the masks, so their mouths become tight and rigid. They are miserable and they take it out on their children because they cannot stand to see their children happy."

"Well, why can't you just tell them all to come here and give them treatments and make them understand? And make them happy?"

"It is not so easy," he said, smiling. Then he nodded to the hospital field. There were dark rings in the yellow grass where the tractor tires had pressed down. "But someday I hope we will have a hospital in that field that will begin to help people. But it is not easy to explain all of this to people. You see, after people have been holding back their emotions for so many years—for so many generations—it becomes a way of life and people accept it. They even think they like it. Life is safer behind the mask."

"Or in the trap," I said. We talked about the trap a lot.

"Ja. Good, Peeps. In the trap. And because it is safer there, people want to remain. They are so accustomed to killing and hating that they spend all their time justifying it and trying to destroy anyone who tells them they may be wrong. They make drugs that suppress the unhappiness and say they have cured it. But the badness is still there, eating them up. They say that I am a quack and that the accumulator is a sex machine. Don't you see, Peter? Man is afraid of the streamings in his legs and he is afraid of life. He is afraid of his basic core of goodness. That is why the FDA has attacked us and is trying to destroy us."

"But the sky isn't afraid, is it? I mean we can help the streamings in the sky and make it better, can't we?"

He nodded and looked around. The sun was just above the treetops, but it was still quiet. I felt a lot better.

"But why is the sky sick?"

"That's a very good question. I'm not sure I fully understand it yet. At first I thought it was all due to Oranur, but since I see trees, plants, and much vegetation dying all the way down to New York, I am not sure any more. Something is killing the atmosphere." He shook his head and pushed his hand through the white hair. "Ja. It is better. Drawing from Zenith helped."

"Is drawing from Zenith like when you make my belly soft?"

He laughed. "Ja. Somewhat. It sort of loosens it. Ja."

He looked at me hard. "You are a good little soldier, Peeps. You are very brave and you must be strong for the battle that may come." He looked at me very hard and his eyes made mine water.

"All right, son." Nodding at the cloudbuster and looking to the mountains, he gave the gentle order, "Now, catch the wind."

A loon warbling across the lake's black water woke me at dawn. I lay shivering in the pale morning light watching the sky change. The loon cried again and again and then there was only shimmering dew.

Soon, before it was fully light, Tom began mowing up by the lab. The low putt of the mower came across the dark wet meadows into the bedroom changing all the time as he mowed in low places and then in high places. I slept.

After breakfast I went into town and borrowed the 16-millimeter projector from the public school. When I finally found Makavejev after I spoke with Vernon Collins, I told him I had some old footage my father took, and he wanted to see it. That evening we tacked a sheet up to the wall in the motel and sat back to watch the movie.

The film had no leader and started very suddenly with me bouncing a big ball in Forest Hills—it must have been 1947—so conscious that Daddy had a camera and was watching me through it.

And then, all of a sudden, I was terribly conscious of the fact that I was Reich's son. Here, sitting in a dark room with a real movie crew looking at a movie—of me!—I felt stupid. Like an object, sitting there, laughing at myself looking at the camera, clowning around. I wondered what they thought of me. Here I had been friends with these strangers because . . . because they liked me? But they had to like me, didn't they? Didn't Makavejev have to be interested in what I told him back in New York? He was making a movie about my father. He wanted information for *his* movie.

The projector rattled on. This must be before 1948 because

we were still living in the upper cabin while the lower cabin was built. Ilse is giving me a bath in a washtub outside the cabin. We are laughing. She dries me in the doorway and our dog, Doggy, comes up and nips at me. I draw away.

What does this movie crew think about this naked child and this person sitting naked and open in the same room with them?

Playing naked, in color now, with a friend at Mooselucmeguntic Lake. Naked at three or four, chasing a sweet naked girl into the water. Now, alone at Orgonon.

Naked. Picking apples. I am older. It is the same apple tree that stands alone up by the road to the lab. Ilse climbs the tree and shakes the branches. I remember the way apples sound falling into the grass. I sit naked in the grass turning an apple over and over in my hand. Was I afraid then?

Makavejev and the cameraman talk in Serbo-Croatian. "We were discussing the way in which Reich holds a camera," Makavejev says. "It is quite interesting. He had a good eye." But I couldn't listen any more because the last scene is with me and Tom. It must be after they tore down Tom's grandfather's barn in 1948, down by the birch tree where we later built the cloud-buster platform. There is a huge pile of old rotted timber we had to take to the dump. The Studebaker pickup is backed up to the pile. A younger, leaner Tom Ross looks uneasily at the camera. You can tell he is listening hard to his new boss, The Doctor, who is telling him what to do. He turns to me. I am wearing striped overalls and grin at the camera. Tom waits as I reach over for a piece of wood from the pile and hand it to him in a slow arc. He takes it from me and throws it in the truck and soon we are together in a real movie, throwing old rotten timbers into the back of the pickup truck. Maybe Makavejev would use that. It is my favorite scene.

If only this movie could capture the irony of Tom's being there, first as the child bringing the cows in down to the barn, then as the man in his early thirties who had just begun to work for the doctor in 1948, tearing down the same barn. And then a few years later he builds the cloudbuster platform practically on top of the foundation of that same barn. And now, at retirement age, he winds his lawnmower around and around the cloudbuster platform and the memory of the old barn.

After the movie, we went over to the Rangeley Inn for a beer. I felt embarrassed that the movie had been all about me; Makavejev wanted footage of Reich. Furthermore, he didn't seem interested in my idea about Tom. I asked him how the movie was coming. He looked into his beer and spoke seriously.

"It is very difficult to say," he said. He must have been curious about how I saw myself fitting into a movie about my father. "It is hard to say how it will go. Right now it is very loose. It is hard to talk with many of the people who worked with your father. Many of them are silent as if they are in shock of some kind. They get very emotional when they talk about certain aspects of Reich. It is as if they have a blind spot."

He looked at me. Was he talking about me? Did he know something I didn't? He talked more about his movie:

"Every man has a deep need for more freedom," he said. "And now the question of armor comes in. As you know, 'The psychological armor is just the psychological part of muscular armor.' It is extremely hard to break the psychological armor. People can participate in something and then go back into their shells. The problem with this film was to make a playful structure that could lose the audience so they can be led. So gradually they are deeper and deeper in places where they never actually voluntarily or consciously go. Step by step they are in some sort of humanistic or fatalistic world but actually they are in touch with the desocialized part of themselves . . . deep sexual feelings. Or fears. Or terrors. Private terrors . . ."

The treatment room is in between the bathroom and the library. It has a blue carpet, the picture of the man with muscles, a medicine cabinet, and pictures in a frame. One of the pictures has Daddy on skis on a mountain and one is when he was a little boy with a rocking horse. I took off my clothes and looked out of the open window to where the warm sun made everything bright. The smell of hay came all the way up the hall and in the window on the wind.

There were funny thin clouds in the sky that I forgot to ask Tom about. Tom always knew when it was going to rain.

When Daddy came in I lay down on the couch. He sat down on the chair and watched me breathe.

"Hi, Peter." He watched me breathing. "How do you feel?"

"I feel okay, I guess."

"Did you have a good morning mowing with Mr. Ross?"

"Yup. We finished the whole field."

He put his hand on my chest and pressed slowly down. His hand felt big and warm. I smiled.

"It is time to be serious. Now let's see. Show me your eyes. Ja. Look at me. All right, now follow my finger. Follow it. That's right, let your eyes go, let go, follow my finger." Following until it turn my eyes until they were tired, sneaky, and surprised. I couldn't any more. "Let go, come on, let them go." Finger dancing all around pulling at my eyes until I squeezed them shut. "Okay. Breathe." I breathed. "Deeper. All the way.

"It is all right. It is all right. Come now, let me see. Have you been stuttering any more, hmm?"

Finger, no thumb, probing up under my chin as if it would come right out in my tongue, hurting, arrrgghhhh

"That's right, that's right. All right, turn over, let me see your neck." Fingers catching my face in the neck and twisting it out into the sheets with hurting and anger ow! More and more, biting into the sheet. "No! No! No! It hurts." Breathing hard, alone.

"Roll over." His voice is gentle, his eyes watch me carefully as I lie breathing. "All right, Peeps, now breathe out, gently."

inbreathingoutbreathingin. oooooph

"Breathe more deeply." He pressed his hand down. I closed my eyes and breathed out until I could feel it down to where his hand was. I smiled.

"Don't run away, Peeps. Breathe. Breathe out."

"I am breathing out. I gotta breathe in sometime!"

His hand pressed down harder and I felt all my air going uuunnhh. Then he let me breathe in but not enough to make it feel tight against my chest before it was ooooph again.

I breathed for a while and then it started to tickle. I giggled.

"Don't laugh, Peeps. That is running away. Breathe out. Let it all out. Don't be afraid to be afraid." His hand, pressing against my stomach, hurting, pressing a belt in my stomach.

"Uuuuuuunnnnnn oh Daddy it hurts. Please, Daddy, please uuuuunnnnnhhhh." My legs, pulling up to hide my stomach from the hands.

"Where is it, Peeps? Don't be afraid. Come on, keep breathing. Let it out. Breathe."

I didn't feel like it. I didn't want to do anything just get away from his hand. It hurt I didn't want it there and grit my teeth and make a face. His hand was up at my throat and unlocking my jaw to let me scream with my face and my legs.

"Kick, Peeps, kick. Kick, now. Ja. Hard, that's right. Kick. Harder, harder! Come on, good. Ja. No, the pillow. Hit the pillow. Ja. Good. Harder, harder, now let it come out."

Gnashing my teeth and kicking twisting to get away the sadness with my legs, the sadness coming up from my legs, and meeting my stomach at his hand the way falling hay met the earth. And I cried because I was so sad for the hay falling down and for the dead deer and the hay falling down behind the mower, falling away from behind the mower blade, and sad that all those people had left us and because Mummy was going to leave us. She did love us. My ears filled up with tears and ran over. I wanted to turn over and cry but Daddy said,

inbreathingoutbreathing

"Where is it, Pete? Come come, where is it? Let it all out.
If you don't breathe it will be worse. Yell. Come on. Yell."
Fingers at my jaw again telling me yelling me wide open and
screaming me until my face was wrapped in the shadows of
my eyes and the folds of my mouth as I cried and cried. His hand
went to the muscles of my legs, to the place where even hay
tickles me when I lie in it, to the muscles of my legs and I said
no don't but he caught it there and then I was kicking with
my whole body, kicking and flipping on that long white scream
like a fish flopping in angry silver flashes.

When kicking stopped and crying stopped his hand was gone
and the belt inside me was gone and when I breathed out it
felt like a black sailboat on a black river in the evening sailing
with the current with the wake glowing and spreading out,
all the way down to my legs.

Breathing, breathing. His hand on my stomach now gently
again, he said, "Is your belly soft now? You should always keep
it soft." And his fingers pressed down to where the breathing
was going in and out by itself now, like a black boat sailing,
softer and softer. He smiled at me. His hand went from my
neck to my knees only it didn't tickle at all. It just felt quiet and
soft and the breathing sailing along with his hand, streaming.

"Good, Peeps. Now breathe."

All by myself I breathe. "Aaaaaaaaaaaaaaaaaaaaaa," lower
and lower until I felt it moving in my legs just like Daddy's
hands.

Daddy said, "Aaaaaaaaaaaaaaa. That's right. Aaaaaaaaaaaaaaaa-
aaaaaaaaaaaaaa."

"AAAaaaaaaaaaaaaaaaaaaaaaaaaaaaaa."

"Aaaaaaaaaaaaaaaaaaaaaaaaaaaaaaaaa."

And then we were both breathing together, smelling the hay.

"Aaaaaaaaaaaaaaaaaaaaaaaaaaaaaaaaa."

Chapter 6

Of him I love day and night I dream'd he was dead,
And I dream'd I went where they had buried
  him I love, but he was not in that place,
And I dream'd I wander'd searching among burial-places
  to find him,
And I found that every place was a burial-place;
The houses full of life were equally full of death
  (this house is now),
The streets, the shipping, the places of amusement, the Chicago, Bos-
  ton, Philadelphia, the Mannhatta, were as full of the dead as of the
  living,
And fuller, O vastly fuller of the dead than of the living;
And what I dream'd I will henceforth tell to every
  person and age,
And I stand henceforth bound to what I dream'd,
And now I am willing to disregard burial-places and
  dispense with them,
And if the memorials of the dead were put up indifferently
  everywhere, even in the room where I eat or sleep,
  I should be satisfied,
And if the corpse of any one I love, or if my own corpse,
  be duly render'd to powder and pour'd
  in the sea, I shall be satisfied,
Or if it be distributed to the winds I shall be satisfied.

WALT WHITMAN

The dreams, a Looney Tunes cartoon version of my childhood,
began after Makavejev left, taking his movie with him.
  They began with half a deer walking up to the cabin door

and rattling at it. And when I went out to open the door I saw the lake had risen and was lapping at the lawn. When I looked into the water I saw the feet of a man who had drowned and was floating upside down.

Only in this dream, I was the drowned man. I had passed through the surface of the water as an image passes in light through film, and in the dream I saw myself sitting, a long time ago, at the edge of the lake at Annecy, coming out of one phantasmagoric anesthesized dream, afraid of another.

The park in Annecy is wide and open with great white mountains towering over it, dipping their peaks into the clouds. I wandered around the park dazed, watching children play, old men at their *jeu de boules*. I watched couples laugh together in the sunlight.

But I was removed from it all, just walking around with my arm in a sling beneath my ski parka, glad that after the tormented dream in the hospital, it was a gentle, sunny afternoon. The doctors and nurses had been very polite. They told me how brave I was to give them the signal like that.

People probably thought I was an escaped patient or something because I had stuffed a box of cookies into the kangaroo pocket of my parka and reached in every so often for a cookie, and my eyes were streaked and red from the crying.

I still didn't know what it was I had dreamt in the hospital. I only knew that there was some other reality going on, on a different plane, and somehow, sliding around in the gas, I had bumped into it. Walking through the park with the empty sleeve of my parka flapping in the wind, I could only think of the tractor and Tom, mowing in the hot sun with Tom all day long, going around and around, watching the horizon until it was burned into my eyes so that in closing them, it was backwards, the trees bright and the sky dark. And then at dusk, still going around and around in smaller and smaller circles, there would be a moment when the trees and the sky were the same shade, separated by a fine light-blue line: the treetops etched against the sky. I knew that there was another boy on another tractor on the other side of the sky, looking back in at me. Was it that person I bumped into in the dream? Or was he in the movie?

At one point in our conversation, Makavejev said to me, "Movies are like tangible dreams, colorful moving shadows. When you turn the light on, it disappears. This is a very powerful fact."

Only for me, the movie kept grinding away with a vengeance after the lights went on. The morning after Makavejev left, the lake began creeping up the hill to drown me. I fled into the back fields of Orgonon, chased by dreams. Why was I even there, at my father's place? Where could I go? Was there any place I could run to and not be implicated in my father's movie?

I walked from fields into forest, arms outstretched to spread apart branches and cobwebs. This was an old part, untouched by Tom's ax, with branches slapping at me, dragging me back. But suddenly I stepped into a clearing. It was an old dump, one I had not discovered before, hidden among dense branches in a remote corner, protected by mosquitoes and a thick blanket of moss and needles. Only a few broken bottles and a rusted iron stove poked up through the earthy brown cover. For a moment the movie was forgotten. I pulled away at the soft earthy blanket that covered the dump. Thin gnarled roots ran through it like veins, holding needles and moss together so that when I pulled it away it rolled back like a huge monster skin. It was like all the dreams I had as a child, a huge blanket of tiny needles coming to cover me up and here I was, pulling it away.

I picked up a stick and began to poke through the black and rotted mass that lay beneath the surface until I saw something sparkle. Reaching carefully into the darkness I pulled out several small glass pipettes. Only the tips were broken and I was curious to know how many there were unbroken. Digging carefully, I uncovered a whole nest of the thin glass rods gathered together in tight broken rows like little shiny soldiers, stacks and stacks of glass pipettes. It gave me goose bumps to find these neat, fairly well preserved remnants of the lab, probably a small part of a load that Tom dumped here in 1952 or 1953, after the Oranur experiment.

With the rows of glass pipettes spread out in front of me, shining brightly, I stopped to rest. It was hot and the mosquitoes were beginning to close in. When I looked down again I saw something I had not seen before and it made my blood run cold.

Panic ran through me as I looked around in disbelief. Where I had torn up the mossy blanket, strands of 16-millimeter film poked out of the rotten earth like plastic ferns.

The movie was right there, all around me on the dump. Real movies. Old movies, all directed by my father.

At first I wanted to run down to a telephone and call Makavejev, to shout to him that the movie was still here, that he should come back and shoot this grand, final, cinematic irony.

I looked down at the film and pulled a strand out of the earth. Sweating and trembling, I held the pale film up to the sun and went into a dream.

After we went to the dump Tom and I drove the green pickup to the post office. Tom always leaves his hand on the gearshift lever where it shakes. He spits tobacco too, and sometimes I put my hand on the gearshift lever too. Someday he says he'll teach me to drive the tractor so I can help him mow.

The post office is green with a black banister. Tom opened our mailbox, which is big because Daddy gets lots of mail. He handed me a red card which meant a package and said, "Hey, Pete, why don't you go to the window and get this package?"

The man gave me a little box and it had my name on it.

Tom said, "What is it?"

"Oh, it's for me," I said.

When we got back to the truck Tom took a bite out of his

tobacco and watched me unwrap the box. I don't know why I was excited because a lot of the doctors or people who come up in the summer send me presents. Once I got an Indian belt.

When the box opened up I took out the white tissue paper that looked like clouds and inside there was a copper-colored saddle ring.

"What is it?" said Tom.

"I don't know, it looks like some kind of a ring."

It was a tiny saddle made out of copper with leather thongs and a western pommel just like a real saddle. The line around the edge of the seat was funny so I pushed back on the pommel and the top of the saddle slid back. Beneath it was a secret compartment.

"Oh, I remember," I said. "A long time ago I was eating Cheerios in the morning and there was a picture of this ring on the back. It said I could get the ring for fifty cents and a boxtop. Mummy gave me the money and I sent it off. But it was a long time ago and I forgot."

I held it up for Tom to look at.

Tom looked at the ring and then he took another bite out of his tobacco.

"Gee whiz. That's a nice ring," he said.

"It glows in the dark," I said.

Tom let me off by the lab and I snuck across the field through the apple orchard sending messages to the cavalry on my new glow-in-the-dark ring. The grass was tall enough so no one could see me as I came up behind the trees around the clearing and moved along the outside edge toward the far end of the clearing in the woods where Daddy was standing in his long white coat, talking.

On hands and knees, the way Toreano taught me, I went all the way around the clearing so I was standing behind him and could look through the leaves and branches and see their faces.

The men and women were sitting on the long brown wooden

benches that Tom made and I helped paint. The clearing was sort of round with trees all around giving shade. The grass was soft green except for the path that led through the trees to the lab, but it was long grass and came up past the bench legs and people's feet as if they were growing there too.

Some of them I had to call doctor because that is what they were. Some were mister but some only had one name like Mickey.

A doctor was Dr. Baker, who was important, and Dr. Raknes from Norway, with a funny accent, Dr. Hoppe from Israel, who came in an airplane and landed at our dock, Dr. Willie, who comes from Texas and has a star on his fence, and Dr. Duval, whose daughter is named Sally, Dr. Tropp is warm and fat, and Dr. Wolfe is not there. Neill comes from Summerhill. Other doctors have names that we always say in a row. Then there were Mummy and Helen and Eva and Gladys and Lois and Grethe, who were taking notes too. Some of them worked in the laboratory with the mice. The mice lived in a special house in special mice boxes. They were all white.

Daddy was standing in front of me in his white coat talking about energy. He was always talking about energy.

Mummy saw me peeking through the leaves and smiled. She waved her hand so no one would see and said, "Go away" with her lips. When I shook my head she shook hers and said, "Be quiet." So I lay in the grass watching people listen and take notes while Daddy talked. He talked a lot when the doctors came in summer for conferences. They came to learn about his discoveries which were important.

I like it when they come because I make them laugh and they like me. Mummy says she is going to send me away to be Jerry Lewis's assistant because I make people laugh so much. But I really don't like to laugh a lot. Mummy says if you laugh too hard it means you are going to cry.

After a while Daddy stopped talking and the people stood

up and started talking and lighting cigarettes. I drew my gun and jumped into the clearing.

"Bang! Bang! Bang!"

Everybody laughed and came over to talk to me. They all wanted to see my glow-in-the-dark ring.

In the dream, I was down at the lake watching soldiers on the other side. There were armies of soldiers filing up and down the hills with uniforms of bright red, blue, and green glinting like swarms of bluebottle flies. While I watched they started coming across the lake, walking on stilts made out of long glass pipettes. There was a boat on the lake and I was in the boat with my mother, looking over the side, trailing my fingers in the water as she rowed back and forth, wondering if I would touch the deer that had drowned.

Once my mother came to visit and one night we were talking about dreams. I told her I had just had a crazy dream about getting out of the Army and my mother chuckled. She said I always had crazy dreams of one sort or another.

"Why in 1952," she said, "Dr. Tropp gave you aureomycin for an illness you had and he didn't tell me it could make you delirious. You were up all night raving about airplanes or something coming to get you and take you away. I was terrified because I didn't know what was happening. 'They are coming! They are coming!' you shouted."

We chuckled about the crazy dream, but I was afraid, because I didn't understand what was science-fiction and what was real. It scared me that as early as 1952—when I was eight—I was having dreams about things coming from the sky to take me away. But even more frightening were reports I had read recently about flying-saucer sightings. In particular, I was alarmed by reports that two of the Apollo missions were allegedly "chased" or "followed" by unidentified flying objects. All records of these encounters was supposedly censored from NASA tapes.

How much could one believe?

It was easy for me to believe in things like flying saucers, even though it made living a "normal life" confusing at times. (When I worked on the desk at the Staten Island *Advance* the switchboard lit up like a Christmas tree one night with reports of a UFO. I was told that to run a story would have alarmed the population, and no mention of the incident appeared in the paper. But it made me wonder about all the books about suppressed Air Force studies in the 1950s, books my father studied closely. It made me wonder about what happened in Arizona in 1954 and made it harder to dismiss it all as some crazy dream or an imaginary conspiracy.) My mother, on the other hand, found it too difficult and for a great many reasons left Orgonon in 1954 and made a new life for herself. I know it was hard. It had to do with being a woman. She said to me and she has said to others that in regard to women's liberation, she always practiced it. Since the age of sixteen she has been financially independent, although without independent income, even when she was living with Reich. "I have always maintained my personal and financial integrity," she said.

And that was why she left. It had to do with personal integrity. I was never faced with the kinds of choices she had to make, but I know that when the going got tough she acted decisively and strongly. If the child in the dreams would not forgive her for leaving, the adult in me would, hoping she too would forgive for the bad times. Some of her dreams were broken too.

But what happened after she left still seemed like science fiction to me now, with the movie over and lights coming on.

Daddy was playing the organ. All the doctors had gone home for supper after the lecture, and now the music came all the way down across the fields and through the trees, slanting down the long afternoon sunbeams to the garden where Mummy was weeding and shaking her head because the deer and rabbits kept eating the lettuce.

"I don't know what we can do about these animals," she said, still shaking her head.

I was keeping guard with my gun and my glow-in-the-dark ring to make sure that no Indians snuck up on us.

"Come on and help me weed," she said.

I put my gun away but kept it right on the edge of the holster so I could draw fast, and started to pull out weeds. Mummy had a big garden that Tom plowed in the spring. Daddy liked little red potatoes and peas and Mummy grew things he liked.

We weeded together and the music from Daddy's organ was like a soft wind. Mummy hummed as she pulled out the long thin green weeds and threw them over the fence that even a deer could jump over.

"Mummy?"

"What?"

"Now that I got this special glow-in-the-dark ring, do you think I could get another pair of cowboy boots?"

"I don't know, Peter, you just had a pair last year. I think this year we'll get regular warm boots. And besides, you said you wanted ski boots." She threw a handful of weeds over the fence and brushed her long black hair back from her face with the back of her hand. "Okay?"

"Aw, I was looking in the Sears and Roebuck catalogue and they've got some really nice cowboy boots. And I can use the same old ski boots for another year. Please?"

"Well, we'll see," she said, and moved over to start weeding under the carrots.

What I really wanted was a two-gun set. But I knew I'd never get it because Daddy bought me this big one-gun holster set. We went to Farmington together and I wanted to buy the two-gun set that I liked but Daddy liked the one-gun set better so he bought it for me. He said it was better. I wished I had gone to Farmington with Mummy. She gets me things I like. Like my old cowboy hat that I got from Sears and Roebuck too.

We weeded for a while listening to Daddy play songs and then we started to go inside. Mummy said, "Why don't you help me set the table?"

"How come we're eating early?"

She passed me the silverware and napkins. "Tonight we are showing a special film of some of the experiments Daddy did last winter."

"What is it about?"

"Oh, it is about the bions and amoebas and things Daddy sees under the microscope. I thought maybe you would like to go to the Rosses' tonight and play with Kathleen. Maybe they will go to the movies in town."

"Please can I come?"

She stirred the pots on the stove and smiled at me. "I don't think so, Peter, you wouldn't be interested because it is mostly pictures of tiny little things from under the microscope."

"Oh, please can't I go? I'll be quiet. I can play with my ring. Besides, I was over at Kathy's last night. Please?"

"Well, we'll see."

So I went to the movie with Mummy.

When we got to the lab where the movie was going to be, it was dark. People were already there and standing around looking at the stars and talking. Daddy had gone back up to the observatory and we were going to pick him up later.

In the afternoon Tom had moved the benches from the clearing in the orchard back into the lab so people could sit and see the movie. The benches were all in rows facing the wall near the door where Tom had put up the screen. I ran back and forth between the benches while Mummy got the projector ready.

Then the doctors started coming in. I said hello and told a few jokes to make them laugh.

When they were all inside and sitting down, one of them got up and started talking about bions and energy. I wasn't interested and went back to the other part of the lab.

The lab is very long and has big picture windows on the side facing the lake. The other side, toward the hill, has little side rooms where they do experiments with the mice and glass tubes and other stuff. All the way around in the back was a room with lots of scientific stuff like jars and slides and glass things. I got into a dark corner where the lights from the big room couldn't reach and pushed back the pommel on the saddle. Where the saddle moved, the secret compartment glowed like a window into a big green ocean. I moved it around. I didn't even know how to write on it. It just glowed in the dark.

I looked at it for a while and wondered if I should send a message. Toreano was probably back at the fort.

The lights in the other room clicked out and the projector started up. As I got up to go back in and watch the movie, my arm hit something in the dark. I reached out and felt around on the table edge until I picked it up. It was a glass magic wand. Daddy used the magic wands to rub in people's hair and put them over machines that counted energy. My hair made the wand crackle in my ear and made the hair on my arms stand up. It didn't do anything to the glow-in-the-dark screen.

I went around the corner slowly so I wouldn't trip over anything and saw the white light from the projector flickering on the screen. The screen was full of small moving little squiggles that were alive, but you could only see them in Daddy's powerful microscope. He let me look through it a lot.

Daddy is a scientist. He is a lot of other things too and wrote a lot of books. And he was a psychiatrist or psychoanalyst, I can never tell all the things with psych apart anyway. He is a teacher, too, and all these people sitting in the movie came to learn from him because he discovered Life Energy. It is in your body and everywhere. If you don't get stiff or tight, it makes you feel good because it flows through you the way it does in a treatment. It is even in little things under the microscope.

The doctor's voice went on and on as he talked about the bions. Every once in a while the picture changed. Then the doctor stopped talking and they all just watched. I went closer so I was right behind the projector watching the reels go around and around but I couldn't see very well.

So I got down on my hands and knees with the magic wand in my hand and started crawling underneath the benches so I could get closer to the screen. Underneath the benches was a forest of legs. Some were crossed and some were tapping on the floor. Some people had their shoes off and their toes wiggled in and out. It all looked funny in the faint flickering light from the projector. I started to laugh but kept on going until I was in the middle of the forest and bumped into a leg. Mickey leaned down and whispered, "Peter, is that you? What are you doing?"

"Shhh," I whispered back, "I'm trying to get closer."

More and more hands started reaching down beneath the benches to feel what was going on. Sometimes a hand patted my back or my head and one scared hand reached down and touched my face. I heard a few people giggle, too.

All of a sudden I bumped into something soft. I felt all around it. It was a hat. So I put the hat on my head and kept on moving past legs until I was in the front row, leaning on my hands watching the silly blobs go around and around while the doctor talked about them. I wished they would show movies that Daddy took of me. They were more interesting than Daddy's blobs. I waved the magic wand to make the blobs go away.

When the movie was over someone turned on the lights and

Mummy started changing the reels. Some of the doctors in the front row leaned over and said, "Hello, Peter, what are you doing here? And what are you doing with that funny hat and the glass rod?"

"This?" I held up the magic wand. "This is a magic wand."

I pulled myself out from underneath the benches and stood up in front of the screen. From a back row, somebody said, "Hey, that's my hat!" But in front of me someone said, "Are you a magician?"

"Yes!"

The hat was squashed down over my eyes. I raised the magic wand and everybody laughed. Somebody clapped.

I waved the wand back and forth and turned around in a circle. "And now, folks, the show is about to begin!" I waved the wand over all of them. "The greatest show on earth is about to begin!"

Everybody laughed and I laughed too. It made me feel good and happy. But then Mummy walked down the side of the benches next to the wall and whispered, "Peter, stop it at once. Don't be a silly fool. Stop it or I shall tell Daddy."

But I just remembered the thing that Bill taught me so I said it, waving the wand: "Yessir, folks, he walks he talks he eats ice cream and he crawls on his belly like a reptile. Step right up, folks, only one thin dime!"

Waving the wand up and down I danced back and forth in front of the benches and everyone was laughing.

Mummy came over to me and held my arm. She took the wand away and said, "All right. Go outside. I warned you." I looked at her and she was mad. Some of the people had stopped laughing so I waved goodbye feeling funny and empty inside.

I went outside and sat on the lab porch. When my eyes got used to the dark I could see the stars. Then I heard the projector start up again and looking through the windows all I could see was the blobs moving around on the screen and I was terribly terribly scared that Mummy was going to tell Daddy.

The lights went out and the movie came on. It wasn't a very good print; the faded garish colors added to the intensity of this 1950s science-fiction spine-tingler, *The Fly*.

Halfway through the movie, just when the monster appears, a freak walks into the theater. He staggers down the aisle stoned out of his skull, freaking on the fly monster. "Aaaaaargh!" he shrieks, pressing his hands to his temples. "Shit! What is this!?"

The movie is about a scientist who has discovered how to send matter through space. He has developed a special kind of box.

When he puts an object in the box and pulls the lever, presto, the object disappears in a puff of smoke and reappears in a similar box at the other end of the lab.

After repeated success sending objects back and forth through space, the scientist decides to send himself. Alas, unnoticed, a common housefly buzzes into the sending box. When the scientist emerges from the other box, molecules have shifted in transmigration. The scientist now has the fly's head and one of his arms. Somewhere, the fly has his.

The film continues after the freak walks in, screams, and takes his seat, building tension around whether or not the scientist will get changed back to a human being before his fly brain takes over his body. The fly, however, manages to escape, and as time passes, the fly's brain begins to rule the scientist's body. Finally, afraid of his own animal instincts, the noble scientist has his wife do him in.

In the last scene, a benevolent uncle comforts the scientist's widow and son. He tells the son that his father had "touched on knowledge of the future," and, "Maybe someday, in many years, the world will understand his contribution," and, "He was ahead of his time."

152

Slowly the scene dissolves. Music up. Lights up. People begin getting out of their seats and walking out of the movie but I sit there dazed and numb. Right there in the movie, people were laughing at how incredible The Fly was when sitting right there in the middle of the crowd was someone who had been through something like that and it was real. It was just more believable in a movie.

What was believable? I still had the magic wand, only now it was a typewriter. It happened. All those things happened but no one believed them. Reich was insane, they said.

But who was to judge? Did flying saucers actually chase Apollo, our astronaut-heroes, streaking toward the moon?

Why are people who live in communities in the Southwest, near former bomb test areas, having epidemics of leukemia and cancer?

When will people understand?

I think what hurts me most, in the most personal way, is that I feel mankind is groping blindly toward some understanding of the great forces at play in the universe and that my father was one of a very few men in history who understood the rhythm, the first to understand the function of the orgasm, things that glow in the dark spontaneously.

But that is still my good soldierly loyalty showing through. I want him to get credit. Does anyone understand?

That was always my trump card: Nobody understood.

I'm not sure my father thought that nobody would ever understand, although he knew it would take a long time. The war, the great misunderstanding, the conspiracy, was on all levels. As long as man's character structure blocked him from life and he acted out that character structure in wars and bureaucracies, he couldn't understand. Understanding—really understanding, about the eyes and the energy—meant more than agreeing and nodding and being a cosmic captain. It meant going through deep emotional changes and incorporating them into one's character.

I *understood* that, but how could I go about living a regular life when a flying saucer might come down any day and pick me up? I don't know what happened in the skies of Arizona in 1954 . . . does anybody? When the argument breaks down, people say, "Well, he was crazy," making insanity the only way to deal with those far-out issues. Hitting below the belt is good American sport. They attacked *him,* not his ideas. "They want my penis," he said. Was he wrong?

And here I am with my magic wand, dancing around in that other movie, feeling guilty now for being that silly clown, the fool, for showing off to the audience. Once at a lecture, he used me to demonstrate a therapeutic technique.

Aaaaaaa.

A tall glass of warm water still milky from the tap. Swallow quickly and then with the forefinger of my left hand, probing down around my tonsils until it comes up and sprays out and twists my mouth. Sometimes when I do it it makes my face feel like the faces in the mental hospitals, twisted, leering, barfing. Again and again until my chest throbs and tingles from the spasms.

Or screaming on a couch, yelling, gagging, vomiting, letting all the muscles run and twist until it breaks loose through my whole body . . . keeping my belly soft.

Isn't that just another authoritarian order, a command I obey too willingly? Is there nothing I can do for my own reasons?

The last thing Makavejev did before he left Rangeley was to tape an interview with me. We went out to the back porch of the motel and sat quietly waiting for the sound man to come. He had to get the tape recorder out of the car that was already packed. When I drove up, they were all packing quickly. Makavejev said there was tension and they decided to get moving. Looking out over Haley Pond, Rangeley's back yard, it seemed a very peaceful June afternoon, a good place to relax. But Makavejev insisted they had to leave.

When the sound man finally came and sat down behind us, with the microphone protruding between us, I got nervous.

It was as if Makavejev were calling my bluff. Sitting there on the back porch of a motel in Rangeley, Makavejev was going to ask me questions and I was—for the first time, really—going to put myself "on record" about . . . about me? My father?

Thousands of moviegoers were going to hear my voice as they watched any number of scenes, depending on Makavejev's whim. What would it be? Was it wrong for me to be in his movie at all?

I waited. Makavejev nodded to the sound man, who pressed a lever on the recorder. Silently, the spools began revolving.

Makavejev leaned forward in his chair, fiddling with his hands as if there were invisible knobs on them and he was tuning me in.

"Could you tell me," he asked, "who you are?"

Driving up to the observatory after the movie to get Daddy, Mummy didn't say a word to me.

I ran up the steps to the study ahead of her and walked into the room quietly, walking around by the bookshelves, running my fingers over the books that went all the way to the ceiling. The room was warm and quiet because the wooden walls and the ceiling had soft lights on them and made Daddy's hair all silvery.

He was sitting at his big desk writing and when he heard me padding on the rug he looked over the tops of his glasses.

"Hi, Peeps," he said. "Where is Mummy?"

"She's coming." I looked down at the floor. If she told him he would get really mad. It was so scary when he got mad. I walked into the library where there was a couch and said, "I guess I'll go to sleep for a while."

Mummy came in and started talking to Daddy. I pretended to be asleep but all of a sudden his footsteps came across the room. My heart pounded all the way into my head.

"Peter." He yelled. I sat up and tried to look sleepy.

"What?"

His face was red and I felt his eyes burning. Mummy was standing in the study next to the light.

"Look at me!"

The carpet in the library was red. If I was sitting in the red chair that we sat in to listen to the Lone Ranger on the radio instead of the couch he wouldn't be mad at me.

"Look at me! You play clown in front of everyone?"

If I squeeze my eyes shut sometimes there is a yellow wave or sparks. I squeezed them shut but it was only a glowing square. It was wrong to play magician at the movies.

"Look at me! You disrupt my movie?"

It was wrong because I laughed too hard and Mummy always said if you laugh too hard you'll cry.

I looked up. His face was swimming in my tears and his eyes reached out and hit me.

"Oh, Daddy."

I stood up and ran over to him and cried with my arms around him. He was warm and the smell of his skin oil came through the roughness of his shirt. Daddy Daddy Daddy Daddy

He stood there in the middle of the library while I cried and then he reached down and picked me up and held me in his big arms.

After I got into bed Mummy came in to say goodnight. I took the ring off and tucked it under my pillow.

"Mummy, I forgot to show Daddy my new ring."

"It's all right. You can show it to him tomorrow." She sat down on the bed and smiled.

"Is he still mad at me?"

"I don't think so." She pulled the covers up to my neck and smoothed my hair back. "But you should remember not to be silly when there are a lot of doctors around. Daddy doesn't like it and you get in the way."

"I'm sorry. I won't do it any more. Are you going to send me away to Jerry Lewis?"

She laughed. "Yes."

"Will you sing me the cowboy song?"

She turned off the light and started to sing.

> Here come the cowboys
> riding on their ponies
>
> They go out to the prairies
> to round up all the cattle
>
> Then they come back to the ranch house
> and put away their ponies
>
> Then they go in to the bunkhouse
> and then they go to sleep
>
> heyup heyup heyup

Waking up, at Annecy, at Orgonon, at the dump, was not the way it was supposed to be. At the end it was supposed to be smooth and quiet, with faint ripples of water spreading out across the lake as the bust of my father moved majestically over the surface of the water. But instead of being smooth and silky, the wake of the bust was like a long undulating zipper, opening the lake, showing me dreams that were nightmares.

It is only a few inches from my face to the water in the toilet. Muscles pull in my jaws and neck, retching. I roll my eyes until the rolling makes my whole face move like a fish groping for water, like a baby, contorted, screaming, vomiting, letting it out as my body shakes in waves and currents, all by itself breathing deeper and deeper. It is easier in a toilet. You can kneel down, breathe more deeply. Aaaaaaaaaaa. Finally, my chest hums.

When I went to an Orgone therapist for help I cried for many reasons. The first reason was that when he put his hand on my chest it wasn't my father's. I miss his hands on my chest. And then after that hand had burned into my lungs, I cried even harder knowing that when the session was over I would have to get up, leave the office, and walk out into the street, alone.

I was afraid. That is why I went; I was afraid of my anger.

I didn't trust myself; there must be anger and bitterness somewhere hidden inside me. But how can I be angry when I am still afraid?

Afraid of flying saucers. Afraid of what it would mean to simply say: My father was right about everything and no one is qualified to say he was wrong.

Because nobody knows.

Why not think that? Why? Am I so politically naïve to think he died of a simple heart attack? He said he was going to be murdered. He said they were going to kill him in prison. He told us he had proof of the conspiracy. Why not think that? Either way, I feel guilty and helpless, afraid of letting him down, afraid of not being faithful enough.

Aaaaaaaa.

Standing up from the toilet, fingers slimy, face smeared, throat chafed and sore from stomach acids . . . what now?

How can such a good faithful soldier walk out the door and be free? You see, I was a real soldier. I really believed all that stuff. I was even in the *real* army, the United States Army. SP4 Ernest P. Reich, US 51522192. I played the game all the way. Yes sir. No sir. There was real security in knowing I had to obey orders.

In a way, I guess, it was my own conspiracy. There were other, secret things going on, and I only let the truth slip out once, during the first week of basic training at Fort Jackson. It was the day when all the new recruits line up to meet the company commander. Our sergeants briefed us over and over on what to do when we went to see the CO.

"Mens. You guys is going in to see the old man. Now first of all, don't say nothing to him. Just walk into his office and say,

'Sir, Private Jones reports.' Then salute in a military manner and wait for him to salute back. DON'T SAY NOTHIN'. Let him talk to you. Got that? When he's through askin' you questions, he'll salute you and that's your signal. You salute him back in a military manner, Melendez, and make a right face. A right face, Plotkins, and exit through the orderly room walkin' in a military manner. Don't try to see who is comin' behind you and how he's doin', just get the hell out and report back to the barracks for a GI party. We got a inspection tomorrow.

"Now listen up. Don't say, 'Private Jones reports, sir,' the way they do in the movies. You ain't John Wayne and you ain't no heroes. That's for sure. You just walk in there and stand at attention lookin' right over his head and say, 'SIR, Private Jones reports.' You got that?"

Sloppy in our fatigues, heads shorn, faces pale, we mumbled, "Yes."

"Yes what?!" he roared.

"Yes, Sergeant."

"I can't hear you!"

"YES, SERGEANT!" we bleated.

So there we were, five platoons strung out across the company area single-file waiting to go in and say good morning to the lieutenant.

As the line inched closer and closer to the ominous door, people got more and more nervous. The whole right side of the line was atwitch as we tried out salutes, mumbling, "Sir, Private Connor reports." "Sir, Private Giordani reports." "Sir, Private Marble reports." "Sir, Private Reich reports." "Private Tompkins reports, sir. . . . Oh shit no. Sir, Private Tompkins reports."

"Hey," someone yelled. "Hey, you guys, where the hell is the right angle supposed to be, under your armpit or next to your head?"

By the time the first Ms were going in I had started to sweat, repeating over and over again, "Sir, Private Reich reports, Sir, Private Reich reports."

The first Ms walked out of the orderly room door with huge sweat stains spreading out from beneath their arms, all pale, washed out, shaking their heads.

Sir, Private Reich reports. Sir, Private Reich reports. Sir, Private Reich reports. Over and over I said it, my arm joining the Ps and the rest of the alphabet twitching toward the door.

Suddenly I was inside. The lieutenant scowled as Plotkin stumbled out into the orderly room.

He sat in his chair stony-faced and looked at me. I looked at him for a few seconds and then drew myself up to attention. Heels together, toes at a forty-five-degree angle, thumb and fingers extending straight out from my forearm which was the hypotenuse of the right angle at my neck and shoulder, I looked over his head and saluted smartly.

"Sir, Captain Reich reports."

After I woke up I ran up the road to meet Tom and go to town for the mail. The rocks on the road hurt my bare feet all the way up the road.

When we got back I rode up to the observatory, waving as we went past the lab. Tom said I couldn't go upstairs because Daddy was talking to some of the doctors so I waited downstairs and played with the ring.

I went into the wing and opened the door to the cellar. The cellar smells like dirt because it is the very bottom of the observatory and the top of the hill. You can see it because there is a big rock right next to the furnace where the hill comes right up out of the ground. When I closed the door it was dark and scary but I wasn't too scared because I could just reach up and open the door. The pommel slipped back easily and the secret compartment began to glow. It was exciting. I could get rings for everybody and write messages. It glowed soft green at me. I wished I knew how to really write messages on it, instead of pretend.

The door opened and Tom looked in.

"Hey. What you doin' down there?"

I held up the ring for Tom to see. "I'm working with my glow-in-the-dark ring. Except I don't know how to write on it. Look."

He turned it over and over in his hand.

"Gee whiz. I don't know either. Maybe it is just supposed to glow." He handed it back. "Why don't you ask your dad. Anyhow, I got to work on the furnace some."

The ring rode my finger up into the hallway and partway up the stairs. The voices of the doctors talking floated down the stairs so the saddle rode down into the big room to wait.

I called it the ballroom because it was so big I thought there should be dances in it. The saddle rode over the tops of the chairs to the fireplace and then around to the big picture window. Next to the window was the walkie-talkie that Daddy used when he wanted to talk to people downstairs.

The saddle rode around to the organ and galloped across the keys to the windows that looked over the pond. The lake was all silvery blue.

Voices came down the stairs loudly and then there were hands on the banister. Dr. Baker, Dr. Duval, and Dr. Raphael came down the stairs. They waved to me and went out the door.

The saddle rode across the ballroom and slowly glided up the wooden banister. Extra quiet like a scout we got to the top of the landing and inched up the last couple of steps to watch Daddy working at his desk. After a while he looked over the tops of his glasses and saw me. He smiled. He wasn't mad any more and I ran across the carpet to him.

"Daddy! Daddy! Look! I got this cowboy ring with a secret compartment just like the Lone Ranger! Look!" I came around the side of the desk and showed him the ring.

He took it from me and looked at it. He frowned.

"Where is the secret compartment?" he said, putting his pen back in the penholder.

I leaned over and slid the pommel back.

"See, it is supposed to glow in the dark and you can write messages on it. Here, cup your hands and you can see it. I want to send messages on it. Could you figure out how to write on it?"

He looked at it for a minute sliding the pommel back and forth. Then he cupped his hand around it to make it glow, but it wasn't dark enough.

"Have you seen it glow in the dark?"

"Sure. I was just down in the cellar and it glowed real bright. Come on down."

"Where did you get it?"

"Don't you remember? A long time ago it was on the back of a Cheerios box and Mummy gave me fifty cents to send away with the box top. It came back in the mail yesterday only . . . only I didn't get to show it to you."

He looked at me seriously, holding onto it so his fingers were right over the pretend stirrups. It was really nice. "Let's just go over to the closet," I said. "You'll see, it really works."

"Peeps, I'm sorry but you cannot keep it."

"What?" He dropped it into his palm. "But I just got it. I'm going to use it with the cavalry to send messages about the Indians!"

"I'm sorry. You can't keep it and that is final."

"But Daddy, I'm sorry about last night. I didn't mean to be silly and make you mad."

"It is not that, Peeps. This glow-in-the-dark substance may harm you. It may be very dangerous. Right now we are preparing an experiment to help us understand it. I'm sorry. I know you like it as a toy, but we must get rid of it. I shall ask Mr. Ross to bury it."

He reached out and pressed the button on the intercom.

"Mr. Ross? Mr. Ross. Please come to the study."

"Bury it? But Daddy, wait. Maybe we can take the glow-in-the-dark stuff out and save the ring. I don't care if it doesn't glow in the dark!" Tears started to blur him and I wiped my arm across my face.

He shook his head. "I'm very sorry, son, but I am afraid the whole ring may be contaminated."

"No fair. I just got it. It was fifty cents. I didn't even get to write a message. Please, Daddy, can't I please keep it?"

"Peter, I am sorry. I have much work to do, preparing lectures, writing articles, and I don't have time to explain it all to you. The substance in that ring is dangerous. Especially when we are making our own experiments. I don't know how this material reacts with Orgone. Now you must understand and go with Mr. Ross. . . . Ah. Mr. Ross."

Tom came in and walked over to the desk. "Yes, Doctor."

"Mr. Ross, please take Peter and help him bury this ring. It may have very dangerous material in it and I don't want him to play with it. Perhaps you can bury it where we have buried some of our other equipment."

He handed the ring to Tom and looked at me.

"All right, Peter. Now I have work to do. Please go with Mr. Ross."

I tried to look angry at him but I couldn't even see him because my eyes were so blurry and mad. He didn't even want to let me play with it a little bit. All he thought about was his energy.

After we buried the ring Tom said I could help him saw wood in the barn but I didn't want to. He walked around the side of the observatory with his shovel and I made the special call.

Toreano came out of the trees on his pony leading mine and we rode down the hill slowly.

I came down the hill running, still running away.

I had been at the tomb, talking to my father. Sitting next to the bust on the huge granite slab looking out over the fields and forests, I talked to the bust for a long time. It was hard to say some of the things I felt. Makavejev was gone. My father was gone. For the first time I felt really alone, at *tabula rasa*, ready for a new reality, a reality that would be better than fantasies. And yet I was still surrounded by my own dreams. The military dream that had been my armor for so long was cracking and softening and I was afraid because I had only reached the surface of things that had been too long buried.

As I talked I examined the bust, running my fingers along the lines that were his hair; long on top, cropped short at the sides and in back. He had a set of hand clippers and liked to clip his own hair, pausing to run his fingers through it in a way that left it standing out at the back as if the wind was always blowing through it.

There had been a thunderstorm during the night and some rainwater was still caught in the rim of one eye. It looked as if the eye was crying. My father was terrified of thunder and lightning. He used to run around and make me hide under tables. Once lightning hit a cloudbuster next to the cabin. Streaks of electricity shot through the house spinning sparks off the wire we used for a radio aerial. My father paced back and forth, afraid. I thought he was afraid that the thunder was directed at him, for understanding it, for being able to play with it. And I guess I have never totally believed that it wasn't, just as I will never be totally sure that a flying saucer won't come and take me away. I just don't know. Perhaps it is the easy way out, keeping one foot in the dream—but it is deeper than that. My childhood is the dream. It is all there, and real.

I brushed the tear away. I didn't like it that the iris and pupil of the eyeball were hollow. In the middle of the eyeball it suddenly fell away and there was a concave hollow. His head is hollow too. Except once some hornets built a huge nest inside his head. I think Tom removed it because the hornets came zooming out and buzzed people who came to look at the tomb. A hero's tomb.

Is it wrong to have heroes? Aren't heroes part of the authoritarian misunderstanding? Or is there a separate, tragic, category? He was plagued all his life for saying things that are gradually being accepted. No one dared to stay with him to discover what lay at the end of his thoughts. Nothing he said has ever been disproved, only dismissed. People attack him for personal reasons . . . me too.

I'm sorry he gave me an attitude toward military authority that was consistent with his paternity (and his century, because in many ways he was a man of the nineteenth century) but inconsistent with his philosophy. I resent it in him that at the end he sought approval and aid from the higher-ups and institutionalized authorities who killed him.

But that is my personal grudge. Perhaps he had no choice at the end. And as Eva said, in a hundred years those personal things won't matter; the important thing is the process, the scientific principles. And until I learn more about what science does not know about Life Energy I have no choice but to believe in everything I experienced as a child. I think my father understood more about the life process than most people are emotionally prepared to accept. And that includes myself. I have a lot of catching up to do and I'm still running. Running away, away from the tomb and down the hill. Running hard, through the hard, new blueberry buds on the side of the hill, across Tom's lawns, down the road to the cabin and past the cabin, Indian paintbrushes and daisies whipping against my legs all the way down to the dock.

Breathing hard and sweating, I stripped and sat on the wooden planks facing out over the water, rising and falling slowly. Way out across the tops of the trees on the other side of the lake Saddleback held the late afternoon sun on its flanks. Clouds reflected in the water were broken up by the bobbing waves and every time it looked as if the reflection of a cloud would reach the dock a wave bobbed up and broke it. I felt confused about how freedom worked—every time I thought I was free of one thing, another popped up.

Splinters of clouds dissolving in the late afternoon sun disappeared and returned. Naked in this silent movement I still felt trapped, afraid of lake monsters beneath the water and terrified of flying saucers from the sky; trapped in the real world.

And guilty. I had armored myself with an incredible military dream which shielded me from the realities of becoming a real person. It was easier to feel guilty and afraid of disobeying the great celestial commands which echoed in all my dreams than it was to grow up. Either way I seemed to lose. I would feel guilty for obeying and for not obeying. Either way I could always, in a human failing, let Him down.

Each time I looked, it was different. But a few things always stayed the same. What always puzzled me about the lake was that wherever you are, the waves always come toward you. But it was still scary. This water was cold and dark out in the middle but if you looked straight down from the dock it was brown and a flaky scummy layer of dead wood and organic matter rose and fell with the heaviness of having already drowned. What happens when you swim without armor?

Being alive means having dreams but without armor. Doing the same thing for different reasons. Keeping my belly soft because I want to, not just because he wanted me to. Standing out there in the middle of my fantasy thirteen years ago, beckoning the lights to take me away, I was not making the energy field and praying because I wanted to go to another planet, it was because I was afraid to stay here. A. S. Neill said to me once, "I am not afraid of dying, I am afraid of not living." And I wasn't even close enough to life to feel that! I hadn't let myself live! I was not seeking life, I was fleeing it. I fled for thirteen years until I stumbled onto this blinding projection of my childhood and here, now, finally, I am looking at it, naked, at the lake.

The waves hypnotized me. It would be easy to just slip in the water and swim slowly out into the brown mud and monsters. Maybe my foot would touch the carcass of a dead deer floating just beneath the surface. I would panic and die breathing water.

Aaaaaaaaaaaaaaa.

The first thirteen years of my life always seemed most real to me, more real than anything that happened afterwards. And now, suddenly, with the infant soldier fading away in the bright lights after the movie, I felt afraid that my life would be empty and lost.

The last thirteen years were lost and unhappy. The infant was frozen in fear inside me, unable to live. I bumped into him in Annecy in a cloudy gassy dream but he eluded me. Three years later, when I was at Rangeley with those friends, he was still a good soldier, defenses strong. It took a movie to break my shell, maybe because movies are so close to dreams and I loved my dreams more than reality. There had been too much sadness; not enough laughter.

As an unhappy adolescent I followed the Playboy ethic assiduously. Big tits. Love 'em and leave 'em. Sex as a diversion, like sports. I fucked a lot. I masturbated a lot, not as a release of energy, but because fantasy was easier to come by than the dream world portrayed in movies. It ran deeper, too, like the lake which only got darker and darker, because being a real person and letting myself love a woman would have meant sharing all that fear. It would have meant sharing who I was, and I was too loyal for that. In my own way, I wanted his penis too.

One night I met a nice girl at a party. We talked for a while and then stopped talking. She was very pretty and her eyes were very deep. After we sat in silence for a while I asked her if she wanted to come to my house.

"To spend the night?" she asked.

I nodded.

She agreed. We came to my house and went into the bedroom. Fully dressed, we fell on the bed. I started to touch her. After a few minutes she said, "I don't want to make love with you."

"Why not?" I asked.

"Because I don't know who you are," she said.

Without thinking, I answered and then knew it was wrong. I felt the scream rising within me, a scream that left me spinning and falling alone, lost in space.

"I'm Wilhelm Reich's son," I said.

Aaaaaaaaaa.

And so I scream and scream. I gag or vomit every morning. Sometimes I scream in the car, driving along lost in the roar of turnpike driving, screaming, letting it out, making the windows vibrate. I need it, it helps me to have a soft belly. It makes me think life is a process of expansion and contraction. It pulsates. There are good things and bad things, but it is always shifting and changing, pulsating. Freedom, an elusive sensation, comes only in sudden spontaneous bursts like the wind that afternoon on the dock, when I was caught between sky and water. It came up suddenly, out of the west when the sun was behind the trees pouring huge sunbeams all over the land. A soft greengolden glow came out onto the smooth lawns that Tom so carefully mowed, and in the sky all the clouds raced away to make it all blue for the wind. And the wind made me shiver in my nakedness. When the sun broke through the trees I dove into the wind following beams of sunlight into darkness. When I burst to the surface I was blinded by the shining water, swimming in the sun's path, bathed in light.

Some of the doctors were dissecting a mouse and I got up real close where I could see his skin all stretched out on the board with pins in him and his organs all purple and smelly.

Some people were working at the row of microscopes and holding glass jars up in the air. I thought of a couple of jokes but didn't feel like making anyone laugh. Around in the back where I found the magic wand, Mummy was sitting on a white lab stool making glass pipettes. I sat on the stool next to her and watched her hold them over the little flame until they turned red, draw them apart, and break them. She looked at me.

"Hello," she said, putting the new pipettes down.

The stool went around faster and faster until I felt myself getting dizzy as I kicked it higher and higher. When I was as high as the table I looked at the little stack of glass pipettes.

"Have you been crying? What's the matter?"

She put her hand out to take a tear away from my cheek. Her fingers were warm from the glass and it made me cry. She pulled me close to her and held me while I cried. She brushed my hair with her warm hand.

"It's okay, Peter, it's okay. Everything will be all right. Now tell me what happened."

I told her what Daddy said and how Tom had helped me bury the ring. She frowned and squeezed me.

"Well, there are some things we just can't have. We didn't know that it was a dangerous ring and if we had, we wouldn't have bought it. It wasn't your fault. And Daddy may be right. It might not be good for you."

"But he wouldn't even let me play with it."

"Well, it is just one of those things. Maybe you will get a pair of cowboy boots for Christmas and that will make up for it. Hmmm?"

She held my face back from her and with her warm thumbs stroked the tears from my eyes. She smiled and I smiled. She hugged me again and said, "All right. Now. I have to make some more pipettes. Do you want to help?"

I helped her put little wads of cotton in the ends of the pipettes and then we made droppers. Mummy took a long piece of glass and heated it in the middle. When it turned red she pulled it apart very slowly until it almost broke and then she took it out of the flame. When it cooled, she broke it and turned it around. She heated the end and just when it began to melt she pressed it against a hard board to make it just a little bit flat at the other end. Then she put the finished pipette in a row. At the other end of the row I picked them up and put rubber nipples on them.

Nipple was a funny word. Mummy had big ones. She told me I used to suck on them for milk. Once I tried to get milk out again but there was none left. I only have little ones. Daddy's are bigger than mine and have hair all over them and smell of his skin oil.

I put one of the rubber nipples in my mouth and tried to suck on it but it didn't taste good.

"What are you doing?" said Mummy.

"I was just sucking on it. You called it a nipple and I wanted to suck it. Will I ever be able to suck yours again?"

She smiled. "No, I don't think so."

I wheeled the stool down until I was dizzy again and walked back through the lab.

I walked into the big room where the movie had been. People were all leaving for lunch, going out the door talking and laughing. Just as I was passing one of the little side rooms where they did experiments, someone said, "Wait for me!" and ran past me out the door. He left the door to the room open so I went in.

The door closed by itself behind me and made the room pitch-dark. It smelled of metal because it smelled of accumulators. There were many accumulators big and small and in the darkness they all smelled of steel wool. One of the accumulators was a twentyfold one which was very strong.

It was pitch-black in the room except for the smell and a small buzz. After a while I could see faint shapes on the counter but I couldn't see where the noise came from. I shuffled through the darkness until I came to a small accumulator where the noise was. The accumulator had a little square window. Inside

the square window crackling very softly was a vacuum tube
and in it, glowing at me in the darkness, was a clear cloud of
blue Orgone Energy.

Mosquitoes were biting badly. I put the faded blue movie film
back on the dump next to the little mound of glass pipettes and
looked at them lying against the cold dark rotten earth. The film
curled gently around the stack of sparkling glass. I pulled more
strands of film out of the earth from wherever it poked out and
threw it on the pile and then I buried it all with moss and pine
needles, roots, and broken bottles and walked back through the
trees into the fields of Orgonon.

It was late afternoon and I walked slowly through the grass
and flowers feeling a peaceful kind of relief. I had the feeling
everything was going to be all right. Look, even after Makavejev
left, the flowers came out, and I walked through a mass of sway-
ing color across the fields: Indian paintbrushes, daisies, and,
hidden beneath their leafy camouflage, wild strawberries.

As I came over the top of a small rise I could see all of
Orgonon: the weedy, overgrown meadows rolling right up to
Tom's bright lawns extending from the laboratory, and barely
visible through tall trees at the top of the hill, the Observatory.
And then moving backward across the green lawn in front of the
lab came Tom's truck. He backed his old red Chevy pickup
right up to the cloudbuster platform and I walked over to see
what he was doing.

When I got there, he had opened the tailgate and was throwing timbers from the platform onto the truck. The cloudbuster
was gone, crated up in the barn. Tom pushed his hat back
on his forehead and explained that the wood was rotten and that
sightseers who came to Orgonon often ignored the "danger"
signs and clambered up the rickety steps to crank the cloudbuster around like a toy.

He shook his head and grinned. "Why, last summer Bea told me I ought to come over here and chain it down. That's right, chain her right down because people was coming up and messing with it all the time." He leaned over and spat a quid of brown tobacco juice onto the grass. "Once some folks came up and messed with it five days in a row and didn't we have rain every day for a week!"

He raised his eyebrows like Groucho and spat some more.

We talked for a while in the late afternoon sun and then I got up on the old platform and started handing pieces of the rotten structure to Tom, who threw them into the bed of the truck.

We stood there together in the late-afternoon sunlight with his old Chevy idling and pouring clouds of blue smoke over us, passing pieces of wood over to the truck slowly and methodically, not talking, just working together. We worked easily together as if we had been doing it for a long time and it was as if the swinging arcs of wood were already there and all our arms had to do was find the place in space where they were.

Soon the truck was nearly full; the platform nearly gone. Soon grass would be growing where the platform had been, but nothing would be forgotten. And when I straightened up to wipe away the sweat I saw that the long golden sunbeams had come down and stretched out across the treetops as the sun sank into shimmering leaves etching brightness against the sky's edge. For an instant I thought I could look across that thin line glowing on the horizon and see through to the other side. I closed my eyes and it was still there, happening again and again, over and over, and I am not afraid of going there now or afraid of having been there. And when I opened my eyes, the light had already gone and I was here.

Tom rested too. He took out his tobacco and took a bite as we watched the dusk settle over Orgonon. He offered the plug to me, grinning. He said,

"Try it. It's good."

Obelisk